Funny Stories for 8 year olds

Helen Paiba was one of the most committed, knowledgeable and acclaimed children's booksellers in Britain. For more than twenty years she owned and ran the Children's Bookshop in Muswell Hill, London, which under her guidance gained a superb reputation for its range of children's books and for the advice available to its customers.

Helen was also involved with the Booksellers Association for many years and served on both its Children's Bookselling Group and the Trade Practices Committee.

In 1995 she was given honorary life membership of the Booksellers Association of Great Britain and Ireland in recognition of her outstanding services to the association and to the book trade. In the same year the Children's Book Circle (sponsored by Books for Children) honoured her with the Eleanor Farjeon Award, given for distinguished service to the world of children's books.

Funny Stories

for **8** year olds

Chosen by Helen Paiba

Illustrated by Alan Snow

MACMILLAN CHILDREN'S BOOKS

For Michael, with love *H. P.*

First published 1998 by Macmillan Children's Books

This edition published 2016 by Macmillan Children's Books
an imprint of Pan Macmillan
The Smithson, 6 Briset Street, London EC1M 5NR
EU representative: Macmillan Publishers Ireland Limited,
Mallard Lodge, Lansdowne Village, Dublin 4
Associated companies throughout the world
www.panmacmillan.com

ISBN 978-1-5098-0501-3

15

A CIP catalogue record for this book is available from
the British Library.

Typeset by SX Composing DTP, Rayleigh, Essex
Printed and bound by CPI Group (UK) Ltd, Croydon CR0 4YY

Contents

UFD

Paul Jennings

You can be the judge. Am I the biggest liar in the world or do I tell the truth? There is one thing for sure – Dad believes me. Anyway, I will leave it up to you. I will tell you what happened and you can make up your own mind.

It all starts one evening about teatime. Dad is cooking the tea and Mum is watching *Sixty Minutes* on television. Suddenly there is a knock on the door. "I'll get it," yells my little brother Matthew. He always runs to be first to the door and first to the telephone. It really gets on my nerves the way he does this.

We hear the sound of Matthew talking to an adult. Then we hear heavy footsteps coming down the hall. Everyone looks up and stares at this man wearing a light blue uniform. He has badges on his chest. One of them is a pair of little wings joined together. On his shoulder is a patch saying "ROYAL AUSTRALIAN AIR FORCE". We have never seen this man before.

"Yes?" says Dad.

"Mr Hutchins?" says the man from the air force.

"Yes," answers Dad.

"Mr Simon Hutchins?"

"No," says Dad pointing at me. "That is Simon Hutchins."

I can feel my face starting to go red. Everyone is looking at me. I think I know what this is about.

"I have come about the UFO," says the man in the uniform.

"UFO?" say Mum and Dad together.

"Yes," answers the bloke in the uniform. "A Mister Simon Hutchins rang the air force and reported a UFO."

Dad looks at me with a fierce expression on his face. He is about to blow his top. "This boy," says Dad slowly, "is the biggest liar in the world. You are wasting your time. He has not seen a UFO. He has dreamed it up. He is always making up the most fantastic stories. I am afraid you have come all this way for nothing."

"Nevertheless," says the man from the air force, "I will have to do a report. Do you mind if I talk to Simon?" Then he holds out his hand to Dad. "My name is Wing Commander Collins."

"Go ahead," says Dad as he shakes Wing Commander Collins' hand. "And after you have finished I will have a talk to Simon myself. A very long talk." He gives me a dirty look. I know that I am in big trouble.

"What's a UFO?" butts in my little brother. Matthew doesn't know anything about anything. He is just a little kid with a big voice.

"It's an unidentified flying object," answers Wing Commander Collins.

"Wow," says Matthew with his mouth hanging open. "A flying saucer. Did you really see a flying saucer?"

"Not exactly," I say. "But I did see a UFO."

Wing Commander Collins sits down at the table and starts writing in a notebook. "What time did you see it?" he asks.

I think for a bit and then I say, "Seven o'clock this morning. I know it was seven because the boom gates on the railway line woke me up. The first train goes through at seven."

The Wing Commander writes this down. I don't know if he believes me or not. It is true though. Those boom gates go flying up after a train has gone through. They end up pointing at the sky. When they hit the buffer they make a terrific crash. They wake me up at seven every morning.

The air force man finishes writing and asks me his next question. "Where did you see it?"

I point through the kitchen window. "Out there. I was in bed and I saw it go past my window."

"How big was it?"

"About one metre."

He looks at me with a funny expression but he does not say anything. He just writes in his

4

book. After a bit more writing he says, "And what colour was it?"

"Black," I answer.

"And what was it made of?"

"Skin," I say. "Skin and hair."

At this point everyone in the room jumps to their feet and yells out, "Skin and hair?" as if they have never heard of skin and hair before.

"Yes," I say.

"And what shape was it?" growls the Commander.

"Dog-shaped. It was dog shaped."

"Dog-shaped?" yells the whole family again. I start to feel as if I am living with a bunch of parrots. They keep repeating everything I say.

"You mean," says the Wing Commander, "that you saw a flying object that was shaped like a dog and covered in skin and hair?"

"No," I answer. "It wasn't a dog-shaped object. It was a dog-shaped dog. A real dog."

The Wing Commander springs to his feet and snaps his book shut. "Good grief," he shouts. "You mean I have come all this way on a

Sunday night just because you looked out of the window and saw a dog?" The Wing Commander is getting mad.

"It was not just a dog," I tell him. "It was alive. And it was flying. It flew past the window and up over the house. It came from down there, down near the railway line."

Everyone looks down the hill but I can tell that no one believes me.

"Did it have wings?" says Matthew.

"No," I yell. "Of course not."

"Or a propeller?" says Dad in a mean voice.

"No," I shout. Tears are starting to come into my eyes. "It was moving its legs. Like it was swimming in the air. Real fast. It was moving its legs and yapping."

The Wing Commander is leaving. He is charging down the hall. Before he goes he turns round and barks at Dad. "You had better teach that boy not to tell lies. Wasting people's time with this nonsense about a flying dog." He goes out and slams the front door behind him.

Mum and Dad and Matthew all stare at me. I can see that they don't believe a word of my story. I run to my bedroom and throw myself on the bed. I can hear Dad shouting from the kitchen. "You are grounded for two months Simon. I am sick of these stupid lies of yours. I am going to teach you a lesson about truthfulness once and for all."

I am sick of being called a liar.

I have tears in my eyes.

Dad comes into the bedroom and looks at me. He can see that I am not faking it. I am very upset. He starts to feel sorry for me. "Come on Simon," he says. "You can't have seen a flying dog. It must have been a reflection in the window or something like that."

"I did," I shout at him. "I saw an unidentified flying dog – a UFD. I'll bet you a thousand dollars that I did."

"You haven't got a thousand dollars," says Dad. "In fact you haven't got any dollars at all."

What he says is true. "All right," I say. "If I prove that there is such a thing as a UFD you have to pay me a thousand dollars. If I can't prove it I will do the washing-up on my own every night for three years."

Dad thinks about this for a while, then he grins and holds out his hand. "OK," he says, "if you prove there is a UFD you get a thousand dollars. If not – three years of washing-up. You have one week to prove it." He thinks that I am going to back down and say that I didn't see the flying dog. But he is wrong.

I shake his hand slowly. I am not feeling too good though. If there is one thing I hate it is the washing-up. I am sure that no more flying dogs are going to appear. I do not have the foggiest where the other one came from. Probably Mars or Venus. I wonder if there is a space ship somewhere looking for it – like in *ET*.

"Come on," says Dad. "Let's go down and get some ice cream for everyone. We only have an hour left before the milk bar closes."

We walk out the drive to Dad's precious new car. It is a Holden Camira. A red one with a big dent in the boot. Dad rubs his hand over the dent and looks unhappy. The dent happened a week earlier and it was not Dad's fault. The boom gates at the railway crossing dropped down in front of the car. Real quick. Dad slammed his foot on the brakes and – kerpow – a yellow Ford ran into the back of our new Camira.

"Ruddy gates," says Dad. He is still rubbing his hand over the dent like it is a personal wound. "Someone ought to report them to the railways. Those gates go up and down like lightning. Don't give you a chance to stop."

Dad is especially sore because there were no witnesses to the accident. No one saw it. If Dad had a witness he might be able to make the owner of the yellow Ford pay up. Now he has to fork out for the repair bill himself.

We drive down towards the milk bar. As we get to the railway crossing I see that there is no sign of any trains. I also see that Mrs Jensen is about to cross the line with her bull-terrier. This bull-terrier is the worst dog in the world. She has it on a long lead. This is good. It means that the vicious animal cannot bite anyone as they walk by.

Mrs Jensen's bull-terrier is called Ripper. This is a good name for the rotten thing. Once it ripped a big hole in my pants. It has also been known to rip holes in people's legs.

Ripper snarls and snaps and tries to get off the lead as Mrs Jensen walks along.

We are driving behind a big truck. The truckie is looking at Mrs Jensen's dog Ripper. He is probably glad to be nice and safe inside his cabin. Suddenly the boom gates fall down in front of the truck. The truckie hits the brakes fast. Dad doesn't hit the brakes at all. Our Camira crashes into the back of the truck with a terrible grinding noise.

Dad groans and hangs his head down on the steering wheel. "Not again," he says. "Not twice in the same month." He looks around and then suddenly thinks of something. "Quick," he yells. "Don't let Mrs Jensen go. She is our witness. She saw the whole thing. Run over and get her."

The truckie is getting out. He is a big tough guy.

"Get Mrs Jensen," yells Dad. "Don't let her go."

I take a couple of steps forward. Ripper is

snarling and snapping. He recognises my leg. He wants to take another bite.

"The dog," I say to Dad feebly. "The dog will bite my leg."

Dad is looking at the truckie. He really is a big bloke.

"Don't argue," says Dad out of the corner of his mouth so that the truckie won't hear. "Get Mrs Jensen."

I walk over to Mrs Jensen and her savage dog. "Dad would like to talk to you," I say. "But please don't bring your dog."

Mrs Jensen is not too sure about this. She does not like me very much. In the end she slips the dog's lead over the end of one of the boom gates so that it cannot get my leg.

A train goes through the crossing and disappears along the track.

The boom gates fly up.

Ripper goes up with the boom gate. It flicks him and his lead high into the sky. Up over the trees and past the kitchen window of our house. His legs are moving like he is swimming in the air. He is yapping as he goes.

On the way home Dad is in a grumpy mood.

He has one dent in the back of the car and another one in the front.

I am grinning my head off. I wonder how I will spend the thousand dollars.

P.S. Ripper lands in our neighbour's swimming pool. He is last seen heading for Darwin as fast as he can go.

Count Bakwerdz on the Carpet

Norman Hunter

In the royal carpet cupboard, where they kept the special red carpet for rolling out to welcome visitors, stood the wicked Count Bakwerdz. And he wasn't there to see if the carpet needed cleaning, which it didn't as the Queen had it swept and brushed and beaten and vacuum-cleaned every other day because she couldn't bear the idea of anything not being as clean as seven whistles and five hospitals, whether it was used or not. And he wasn't there to measure it in metres to make sure it had enough yards to go round, or rather go down the steps in front of the palace. Oh no. He was there for a low-down dastardly reason. He was tampering with the royal carpet, which is one of the dastardliest things you can do in Incrediblania.

"Ha, ha, he, ho, ho!" chuckled the wicked Count under his breath in case anyone was listening at the keyhole, which they couldn't have been as there wasn't one, and anyway whoever would want to listen at the keyhole of a carpet cupboard? "He, he!" he chuckled again. "That will do the trick nicely. That will put the King and Queen in a fix when their imperial visitors arrive." And he crept craftily away leaving the royal carpet all secretly tampered with.

Next morning the King of Incrediblania glanced out of the window to see if the postman was coming as he was expecting a nice expensive birthday present from his cousin, the Countess Gillian. It wasn't his birthday yet, but Cousin Gillian always sent birthday presents a bit early because she'd been born rather sooner than she'd expected, and couldn't bear the idea of being late for someone else's birthday.

"Oh my goodness!" cried the King, clapping

his hand to his head, forgetting he had a piece of toast and marmalade in it. "Help, disaster, SOS and everything. Their Extreme Altitudes the Emperor and Empress of Snootistan have arrived!"

"But they aren't due until tomorrow," said the Queen, snatching the toast and marmalade off the King's forehead and jamming them into the wastepaper basket with the gas bill. "We aren't ready to receive them. Whatever shall we do?"

"I know, I know, I don't know!" shouted the King, running round in ovals as the room was the wrong shape for running round in circles. "Quick, quick, summon everybody! Get royal reception committee ready. Lay out royal red carpet, call out the guard, clean the windows!"

And the Queen dashed out crying, "Put the kettle on, dust the sideboard, change your socks everybody, hurry, hurry!"

The dastardly Count Bakwerdz was to blame. It was he who had caused the Emperor and Empress to arrive a day too soon. But how had he done it? By tampering with the royal red carpet? No, no, you can't get imperial visitors to arrive too soon however much you tamper with royal carpets. No, it was the royal calendar he'd tampered with as well. He'd put the sheet of dates for the wrong month on the calendar, but left the name of the right month at the top, and you can't get much more dastardly than that, can you? And because of that the King and Queen thought today was the sixth when it was really the seventh. They ought to have suspected something really because they'd had sausages for breakfast and they only had sausages for breakfast on the seventh of the month; the sixth was scrambled egg day. But how can kings and queens be expected to remember things like that with frightfully important emperors and empresses approaching a day too soon and nothing ready for them? Of course the Cook should have known it was the day of the Emperor's visit. The wicked Count hadn't tampered with her calendar, because he couldn't get into the kitchen without helping with the washing up, and he felt that was too undignified for a count. But oh dear, the Cook's calendar was a year-before-last one that she'd kept because she liked the picture on it.

The King was as white as a sheet just washed with super biological washing powder, except for a black streak down his nose where a speck of dust he'd wiped off the throne had stuck to his finger and come off on his face.

"Disaster, disaster!" shrieked the Queen, going whiter still as she had no black marks on her face. "The Emperor and Empress here and no red carpet down." She made a dash for the bell to ring for a hundred servants. The King dashed at it too and they kept dabbing each other's hands before they could get the bell push pushed.

"Emperor and -Ess coming!" shouted the king. "Get red carpet down steps. Hurry!"

"Tell Cook to take extra pint milk, large loaf instead of small, wash best china, polish silver," gabbled the Queen. She took a rapid look in the mirror to make sure she looked fetching, saw spots on her nose that were really on the mirror, and shot up to the purple bathroom for a quick dab with a sponge.

Before she could decide whether the spots had blown off on the way upstairs, the Lord Chamberlain burst in on the King.

"Men who put carpet down having tea with their aunties," he gasped.

"Bother aunties," spluttered the King. (He had twenty-five assorted aunties of his own.) "Must get carpet down or everything terrible!" He was too frantic to say all of his words.

"Shall lay carpet own self, Majesty," cried the Lord Chamberlain, as he dashed out.

The King rushed round the room tearing his hair out with one hand and putting ornaments straight with the other. The Queen returned from the bathroom, saw the black mark on his nose, and wondered why he should have a smut on *his* nose just because she had seen spots on her own that weren't there.

The Lord Chamberlain grabbed some more footmen and between them they pulled the royal red carpet from the royal carpet cupboard, dragged it down and out at the front door.

The Emperor's carriage drew up at the bottom of the palace steps with imperial creakings and shoutings of "Woa" just as the Lord Chamberlain and the footmen lugged the red carpet to the top of the enormous flight of steps leading down from the palace.

"Just'n time," gasped the Lord Chamberlain. He grasped the end of the carpet and gave the roll a mighty push. Down went the huge roll of carpet, *bumpetty, bouncetty, bump*. But horrors! Disaster! Oo terribly er! A little spare bit of carpet came off in the Lord Chamberlain's hand and the whole great roll of carpet went bounding and bouncing uncontrolled down the steps, straight at the Emperor and Empress, who were just getting sedately out of the carriage.

"Ha, ha," chuckled Count Bakwerdz, watching from his grim, grey castle across the river. "My plot succeeds. The Emperor and Empress will be furious with the King. They'll threaten war. But I shall dash up and rescue them from the runaway carpet and claim the throne. How clever of me to cut that odd bit off the carpet and so let it loose on the Emperor." He dashed down to the river and rowed across just as the Emperor's coach drew away and the great roll of carpet came bounding down on the Emperor and Empress.

But ha! One of the Royal Incrediblanian Guards leapt at the runaway carpet and grabbed the end of it. The carpet went bounding on, unrolling as it went down the steps and across the courtyard, past the Emperor and Empress, who stepped gracefully on to it. But before they could start going up the steps to the palace the Lord Chamberlain came tearing down to try to grab the carpet, and knocked the Royal Guard over before he could stop himself.

Horrors and disaster! The end of the carpet, let loose, started rolling itself up. Down it rolled on the Emperor and Empress, knocked them over and went on rolling with their Extreme Altitudes all wrapped up in it like the jam in a Swiss roll. Now the rampant carpet was all rolled up from its opposite end, and on it rushed down the hill towards the river with the Emperor and Empress inside it.

"Stop that carpet!" roared the King. "Call out the guard, fetch the carpet-stoppers!"

On bounced and rolled and rumbled the runaway carpet. The townspeople joined in the chase. The guards turned out and one rather newish one, who'd put his armour on upside down in the hurry, fell into a ditch and thought he'd better stay there out of the way.

Down by the river Count Bakwerdz grabbed a bicycle that didn't belong to him and went riding to meet the carpet.

"Ha, ha!" he growled. "This is better than I

expected. Now I can stop the carpet, rescue the Emperor and Empress, and say it was a plot to kill them that I have foiled. Then with their help I shall seize the kingdom of Incrediblania." He rang his bell, fell off the bicycle, clambered on again and pedalled off towards the rampaging carpet.

On and on rushed the carpet with imperial feet sticking out at one end and imperial heads out at the other. The Lord Chamberlain leapt on a horse to give chase, but fell off again as he didn't know how to ride.

"Call out the lifeboat!" yelled the King. "Their Altitudes will be drowned when the carpet goes into the river."

On went the non-stop carpet, and after it pell-mell, ding-dong, thumpetty-thump, what's-its-name for leather went the towns-people, the guards, the Lord Chamberlain, and the King and Queen. It zoomed down hills and round squares, into "No Entry" streets and out of "No Exit" ones, past the police station, the railway station, the fire station and the stationers. It took no notice of policemen with their hands up. It ignored notices that said

"Stop", or "Diversion", or "Road Up".

"The river, the river!" roared the crowd. "It's going into the river."

Bouncetty, zoom, thump. The runaway carpet rolled on to the river's edge just as the wicked Count Bakwerdz rode up on his stolen bicycle.

"To the rescue of Their Altitudes!" he shouted, and pedalled in front of the rolling carpet.

Bong, thump, wow! The careering carpet hit the Count's bicycle and knocked it clean over the edge right into the river, Count and all. Then it stopped, right on the brinkmost brink of the wet water.

The crowd came surging up. The Lord Chamberlain and the guards carefully unrolled the carpet and let the Emperor and Empress out. The nervous guard with his armour upside down crawled out of the ditch and went home to tea.

The Emperor staggered to his feet helped by the King.

"Your Altitude," said the King, "what can I say?"

The Empress pushed aside the guards who were trying to help her and got up by herself.

They both looked at the King and Queen.

A distant rumble of thunder was heard.

Five volcanoes erupted in far distant lands.

An eclipse of the sun came on a fortnight too soon where nobody could see it.

The wicked Count Bakwerdz, crawling sopping wet out of the river, didn't wring his hands. He wrang himself out. And he gloated a soaking wet gloat.

"Ha, ha," he growled, "I've done it this time. Even though I didn't succeed in rescuing them and so get them on my side, they'll make war on Incrediblania and I can join them and be appointed Governor General when they've won."

The King was stupefied, aghast, non-plussed, horrified and desperate, all at once.

The Queen wrung her hands, rolled her eyes, shook her head and wished she was somewhere else.

"There's going to be war," groaned the King to himself. "Their Altitudes will be furious, fierce, fiery and frantically ferocious,

I know they will. All is lost. Oh, oh, oh!"

Then His Extreme Altitude the Emperor of Snootistan spoke.

"My word, old chap," he said, "that was a bit of a do and no mistake. Never had such an experience in me life, by Jove! Thoroughly enjoyed it!"

"Me too," said the Empress, shaking carpet fluff out of her hair-do. "Ha, ha, wait till I tell my friends. They'll be apple-green with envy."

The King's mouth opened, but he didn't say anything. Words not only failed him, they disappeared round the nearest corner. Then he recovered a bit.

"You mean you're not annoyed at being rolled down the streets in a carpet?" he gasped. "You mean you aren't going to declare war on us?"

"My word, rather not," said the Emperor. "Don't like wars y'know. Interfere with the sports fixtures and all that."

"And wars mean rationing," said the Empress. "No cream buns for tea. Too disaster-making."

"But how can we apologize?" asked the

King. "How can we make up to Your Altitudes for this indignity, this terrible er er er . . . ?"

"Not to worry," said the Emperor. "If it was a mistake you couldn't help it, and if you did it on purpose it was great fun."

"Was anything said about a banquet?" enquired the Empress.

"Of course!" cried the King. He waved his hands. "To the banqueting hall. Let there be celebrations to welcome Their Extreme Altitudes the Emperor and Empress of Snootistan."

And a tremendously good time was had by all except the wicked Count Bakwerdz, who not only saw his plans in ruins, but had to be pegged out on his own clothes line to dry off and so couldn't go to the banquet.

"A million curses," he growled.

Then the clothes line broke and dropped him into the muddy puddle that the drips from his clothes had made.

Bad News Bear

Anne Fine

I'm not a total lame-brain. Nor am I intergalactically stupid. And I don't go wimp-eyed and soggy-nosed when bad things happen to me. But I confess, as I looked round the dismal swamp that was to be my new classroom, I did feel a little bit cheesy. Oh, yes. I was one definite Bad News Bear.

"Lovely news, everyone!"

Miss Tate clapped her hands and turned to the lines of dim-bulbs staring at me over their grubby little desks.

"We have somebody new this term," she said. "Isn't that nice?" She beamed. "And here he is. He's just flown in from America and his name is Howard Chester."

"Chester Howard," I corrected her.

But she wasn't listening. She was busy craning round the room, searching for a spare desk. And I couldn't be bothered to say it again. I reckoned she was probably bright enough to pick it up in time. So I just carried my stuff over to the empty desk she was pointing towards, in the back row.

"And that's Joe Gardener beside you," Miss Tate cooed after me.

"Hi, Gardener Joe," I muttered, as I sat down.

It was a joke. But he was clearly even more of a bean-brain than Miss Tate.

"Not Gardener Joe," he whispered. "Joe Gardener."

I didn't have the energy to explain.

"Oh. Right," I said. And my spirits sank straight in my boots, setting a personal (and possibly a world) record for getting to hate a new school. I've moved more times than you've watched *Sesame Street*. I've managed bookish schools, and sporty schools, and schools where the teachers keep hunkering down to your level to look you in the eye and ask you how you *really feel*. I even managed four months in a school where no one else spoke English. But I never took against a place so fast as I took against Walbottle Manor (Mixed).

Some Manor! I reckon the building was designed by someone who was taking a rest from doing morgues and abattoirs. The walls were shiny brown and shiny green. (The shiny made it worse.) The windows hadn't been washed since 1643. And all the paintings pinned up round the room looked like eight sorts of pig dribble.

But, hey. Nowhere's *perfect*.

I gave Gardener Joe a nudge.

"So what's she like?"

"Who?"

I nodded towards the front.

"Her, of course. Crock at the top."

He stared at me.

"Miss Tate? She's very nice."

My turn to stare. Was my new neighbour touched with the feather of madness, or what? Here was this epic windbag, droning on and on about whose turn it was to be the blackboard monitor, or some other such great thrill, and Gardener Joe was sticking up for her. I knew right away that this was the sort of school where everyone lines up quietly to do something really exciting, like opening the door for a teacher. And if you gave them something wild to play with, like a wobbly chair, they'd probably be happy all through break.

I looked at my watch.

"Six hours," I muttered bleakly. "Six whole hours!"

Joe Gardener turned my way.

"Six hours till what?"

"Till I can complain to my mother," I explained.

"Complain?"

"About this place."

His face crumpled up in bewilderment.

"But why complain?"

And he was right, of course. Why bother to complain? It never gets me anywhere.

"Marry the woman, marry the job," my father always says.

"But I didn't marry her. You did," I point out to him. "So why should *I* suffer?"

"It could be worse," he warns. "Your mother could get fired. Then we might be stuck here for ever."

That usually snaps me out of it pretty fast.

"You'll like it here," this Joe was telling me. "We do a lot of art."

I stared at the pig dribble pictures.

"Oh. Very nice."

"And we have fun at break."

"Watching the puddles dry?"

Joe's puzzled look came back to take another quick bow. And then he finished up, "And we have singing on Fridays."

"No kidding? Not sure I can wait that long."

But this Joe Gardener was turning out to be a bit of a sarcasm-free zone.

"I feel that way sometimes myself," he said. "But wait and see. It'll come round so fast."

His eyes shone as if he were talking about his birthday, or Christmas.

"Singing on Fridays," I said. "Right. I'll remember that when things get grim." And I looked up to see how we were doing with today's great excitement – choosing the blackboard monitor.

"So that's agreed, then, is it?" Miss Tate was saying. "Flora this week, and Ben the week after."

I suppose, when something of world-shattering importance like this is decided, it's always best to check things one last time.

"Everyone happy with that?"

I'd have put money on the fact that no dill-brain in the world could give a flying crumpet who was blackboard monitor, this week or next. But – whoa there! I was wrong. Quite wrong.

This hand beside me shoots up in the air.

"Miss Tate?"

"Yes, dear?"

"I think it would be nice if Howard—"

"*Chester*," I couldn't help correcting.

But he wasn't listening. He was busy fixing my life.

"If Howard was made blackboard monitor. Because he's new. And I don't think he's very sure he's going to like it here. Because he's already worked out that it's six whole hours—"

See my eyes pop? But what was staggering

me most was that this bozo meant well! He was trying to be *kind*!

"Till he gets home."

I flicked on all exterminator rays, but nothing could stop him. He was being *nice*.

"So I think it would be a really good idea if we made him blackboard monitor."

Joe sat back, satisfied.

Miss Tate spread her hands like someone glowing in a holy painting.

"Flora? Ben? Would you mind?"

Surprise, surprise! Ben didn't burst into tears, and Flora didn't gnash her teeth at not being blackboard monitor for one more week.

So, that's it. Ten minutes in, and I'm head Wiperoony. What Great Luck!

"Well!" Miss Tate said brightly, giving me a meaningful smile. "My blackboard looks as if it could do with a thorough good wiping, just to start the day."

I sighed. I stood up. What else could I do? I took the little furry wooden block from Flora's outstretched hand, and smiled back sweetly when she smiled at me. I wiped the

board, then set the little furry thing carefully on its ledge.

"Very good," Miss Tate said. "Excellent. A lovely job."

You'd have thought that I'd balanced the budget, or something.

Modestly, I wiped the chalk dust from my fingertips.

"And now let's give Howard a nice big round of applause as he goes back to his desk."

I didn't put up any further fight. Chester. Howard. What's in a name? I was a broken reed, ready to slip my head in a noose, or walk the plank, or do anything I was asked. Don't get the wrong end of the stick. I am no wimp. I've smacked heads in my time. Young Chester Howard here has stuck up for himself in schools where the pudding plates go flying, and schools where, if you don't watch yourself, someone's infected teeth are in your leg, and schools where the staff need cattle prods.

But Walbottle Manor (Mixed)! Their sheer bloodcurdling *niceness* had defeated me, and I ran up the white flag.

Howard it was.

Laughing Gas

P. L. Travers

Magical Mary Poppins arrived "out of the blue" at the home of the Banks family when they were desperate for a nanny to look after Jane, Michael and the twins. Life with Mary Poppins is sometimes strange, but it is certainly never dull!

"**A**re you quite sure he will be at home?" said Jane, as they got off the bus, she and Michael and Mary Poppins.

"Would my uncle ask me to bring you to tea if he intended to go out, I'd like to know?" said Mary Poppins, who was evidently very offended by the question. She was wearing her blue coat with silver buttons and a blue hat to match, and on the days when she wore these it was the easiest thing in the world to offend her.

All three of them were on the way to pay a visit to Mary Poppins' uncle, Mr Wigg, and Jane and Michael had looked forward to the trip for so long that they were more than half afraid that Mr Wigg might not be in, after all.

"Why is he called Mr Wigg – does he wear one?" asked Michael, hurrying along beside Mary Poppins.

"He is called Mr Wigg because Mr Wigg is his name. And he doesn't wear one. He is bald," said Mary Poppins. "And if I have any more questions we will just go Back Home." And she sniffed her usual sniff of displeasure.

Jane and Michael looked at each other and frowned. And the frown meant: "Don't let's ask her anything else or we'll never get there."

Mary Poppins put her hat straight at the Tobacconist's Shop at the corner. It had one of those curious windows where there seem to be three of you instead of one, so that if you look long enough at them you begin to feel you are not yourself but a whole crowd of somebody else. Mary Poppins sighed with pleasure, however, when she saw three of herself, each wearing a blue coat with silver buttons and a blue hat to match. She thought it was such a lovely sight that she wished there had been a dozen of her or even thirty. The more Mary Poppins the better.

"Come along," she said sternly, as though they had kept *her* waiting. Then they turned the corner and pulled the bell of Number Three, Robertson Road. Jane and Michael could hear it faintly echoing from a long way away and they knew that in one minute, or two at the most, they would be having tea with Mary Poppins' uncle, Mr Wigg, for the first time ever.

"If he's in, of course," Jane said to Michael in a whisper.

At that moment the door flew open and a thin, watery-looking lady appeared.

"Is he in?" said Michael quickly.

"I'll thank you," said Mary Poppins, giving him a terrible glance, "to let *me* do the talking."

"How do you do, Mrs Wigg," said Jane politely.

"Mrs Wigg!" said the thin lady, in a voice even thinner than herself. "How dare you call me Mrs Wigg? No, thank you! I'm plain Miss Persimmon *and* proud of it. Mrs Wigg indeed!" She seemed to be quite upset, and they thought Mr Wigg must be a very odd person if Miss Persimmon was so glad not to be Mrs Wigg.

"Straight up and first door on the landing," said Miss Persimmon, and she went hurrying away down the passage saying: "Mrs Wigg indeed!" to herself in a high, thin, outraged voice.

Jane and Michael followed Mary Poppins upstairs. Mary Poppins knocked at the door.

"Come in! Come in! And welcome!" called a loud, cheery voice from inside. Jane's heart was pitter-pattering with excitement.

"He *is* in!" she signalled to Michael with a look.

Mary Poppins opened the door and pushed them in front of her. A large cheerful room lay before them. At one end of it a fire was burning brightly and in the centre stood an enormous table laid for tea – four cups and saucers, piles of bread and butter, crumpets, coconut cakes and a large plum cake with pink icing.

"Well, this is indeed a Pleasure," a huge voice greeted them, and Jane and Michael looked round for its owner. He was nowhere to be seen. The room appeared to be quite empty. Then they heard Mary Poppins saying crossly:

"Oh, Uncle Albert – not *again*? It's not your birthday, is it?"

And as she spoke she looked up at the ceiling. Jane and Michael looked up too and to their surprise saw a round, fat, bald man who was hanging in the air without holding on to anything. Indeed, he appeared to be *sitting* on the air, for his legs were crossed and he had just put down the newspaper which he had been reading when they came in.

"My dear," said Mr Wigg, smiling down at the children, and looking apologetically at Mary Poppins, "I'm very sorry, but I'm afraid it *is* my birthday."

"Tch, tch, tch!" said Mary Poppins.

"I only remembered last night and there was no time then to sent you a postcard asking you to come another day. Very distressing, isn't it?" he said, looking down at Jane and Michael.

"I can see you're rather surprised," said Mr Wigg. And, indeed, their mouths were so wide open with astonishment that Mr Wigg, if he had been a little smaller, might almost have fallen into one of them.

"I'd better explain, I think," Mr Wigg went on calmly. "You see, it's this way. I'm a cheerful sort of man and very disposed to laughter. You wouldn't believe, either of you, the number of things that strike me as being funny. I can laugh at pretty nearly everything, I can."

And with that Mr Wigg began to bob up and down, shaking with laughter at the thought of his own cheerfulness.

"Uncle Albert!" said Mary Poppins, and Mr Wigg stopped laughing with a jerk.

"Oh, beg pardon, my dear. Where was I? Oh, yes. Well, the funny thing about me is – all

right, Mary, I won't laugh if I can help it! –
that whenever my birthday falls on a Friday,
well, it's all up with me. Absolutely U.P.," said
Mr Wigg.

"But why—" began Jane.

"But how—?" began Michael.

"Well, you see, if I laugh on that particular
day I become so filled with Laughing Gas that
I simply can't keep on the ground. Even if I
smile it happens. The first funny thought, and
I'm up like a balloon. And until I can think of
something serious I can't get down again." Mr
Wigg began to chuckle at that, but he caught
sight of Mary Poppins' face and stopped the
chuckle, and continued: "It's awkward, of
course, but not unpleasant. Never happens to
either of you, I suppose?"

Jane and Michael shook their heads.

"No, I thought not. It seems to be my own
special habit. Once, after I'd been to the
Circus the night before, I laughed so much
that – would you believe it? – I was up here
for a whole twelve hours, and couldn't get
down till the last stroke of midnight.
Then, of course, I came down with a flop

because it was Saturday and not my birthday any more. It's rather odd, isn't it? Not to say funny?

"And now here it is Friday again and my birthday, and you two and Mary P to visit me. Oh, Lordy, Lordy, don't make me laugh, I beg of you——" But although Jane and Michael had done nothing very amusing, except to stare at him in astonishment, Mr Wigg began to laugh again loudly, and as he laughed he went bouncing and bobbing about in the air, with the newspaper rattling in his hand and his spectacles half on and half off his nose.

He looked so comic, floundering in the air like a great human bubble, clutching at the ceiling sometimes and sometimes at the gas-bracket as he passed it, that Jane and Michael, though they were trying hard to be polite, just couldn't help doing what they did. They laughed. *And* they laughed. They shut their mouths tight to prevent the laughter escaping, but that didn't do any good. And presently they were rolling over and over on the floor, squealing and shrieking with laughter.

"Really!" said Mary Poppins. "Really, *such* behaviour!"

"I can't help it, I can't help it!" shrieked Michael, as he rolled into the fender. "It's so terribly funny. Oh, Jane, *isn't* it funny?"

Jane did not reply, for a curious thing was happening to her. As she laughed she felt herself growing lighter and lighter, just as though she were being pumped full of air. It was a curious and delicious feeling and it made her want to laugh all the more. And then suddenly, with a bouncing bound, she felt herself jumping through the air. Michael, to his astonishment, saw her go soaring up through the room. With a little bump her head touched the ceiling and then she went bouncing along it till she reached Mr Wigg.

"*Well!*" said Mr Wigg, looking very surprised indeed. "Don't tell me it's *your* birthday, too?" Jane shook her head.

"It's not? Then this Laughing Gas must be catching! Hi – whoa, there, look out for the mantelpiece!" This was to Michael, who had suddenly risen from the floor and was swooping through the air, roaring with laughter, and just grazing the china ornaments on the mantelpiece as he passed. He landed with a bounce right on Mr Wigg's knee.

"How do you do," said Mr Wigg, heartily shaking Michael by the hand. "I call this really friendly of you – bless my soul, I do! To come up to me since I couldn't come down to you – eh?" And then he and Michael looked at each other and flung back their heads and simply howled with laughter.

"I say," said Mr Wigg to Jane, as he wiped his eyes. "You'll be thinking I have the worst manners in the world. You're standing and you ought to be sitting – a nice young lady like you. I'm afraid I can't offer you a chair up here, but I think you'll find the air quite comfortable to sit on. I do."

Jane tried it and found she could sit down quite comfortably on the air. She took off her hat and laid it down beside her and it hung there in space without any support at all.

"That's right," said Mr Wigg. Then he turned and looked down at Mary Poppins.

"Well, Mary, we're fixed. And now I can

enquire about *you*, my dear. I must say, I am very glad to welcome you and my two young friends here today. – Why, Mary, you're frowning. I'm afraid you don't approve of – er – all this."

He waved his hand at Jane and Michael, and said hurriedly:

"I apologise, Mary, my dear. But you know how it is with me. Still, I must say I never thought my two young friends here would catch it, really I didn't, Mary! I suppose I should have asked them for another day or tried to think of something sad or something—"

"Well, I must say," said Mary Poppins primly, "that I have never in my life seen such a sight. And at your age, Uncle—"

"Mary Poppins, Mary Poppins, do come up!" interrupted Michael. "Think of something funny and you'll find it's quite easy."

"Ah, now do, Mary!" said Mr Wigg persuasively.

"We're lonely up here without you!" said Jane, and held out her arms towards Mary Poppins. "*Do* think of something funny!"

"Ah, *she* doesn't need to," said Mr Wigg sighing.

"She can come up if she wants to, even without laughing – and she knows it." And he looked mysteriously and secretly at Mary Poppins as she stood down there on the hearthrug.

"Well," said Mary Poppins, "it's all very silly and undignified, but, since you're all up there and don't seem able to get down, I suppose I'd better come up, too."

With that, to the surprise of Jane and Michael, she put her hands down at her sides and without a laugh, without even the faintest glimmer of a smile, she shot up through the air and sat down beside Jane.

"How many times, I should like to know," she said snappily, "have I told you to take off your coat when you come into a hot room?" And she unbuttoned Jane's coat and laid it neatly on the air beside the hat.

"That's right, Mary, that's right," said Mr Wigg contentedly, as he leant down and put his spectacles on the mantelpiece. "Now we're all comfortable—"

"There's comfort *and* comfort," sniffed Mary Poppins.

"And we can have tea," Mr Wigg went on, apparently not noticing her remark. And then a startled look came over his face.

"My goodness!" he said. "How dreadful! I've just realised – the table's down there and we're up here. What *are* we going to do? We're here and it's there. It's an awful tragedy – awful! But oh, it's terribly comic!" And he hid his face in his handkerchief and laughed loudly into it. Jane and Michael, though they did not want to miss the crumpets and the cakes, couldn't help laughing too, because Mr Wigg's mirth was so infectious.

Mr Wigg dried his eyes.

"There's only one thing for it," he said. "We must think of something serious. Something sad, very sad. And then we shall be able to get down. Now – one, two, three! Something *very* sad, mind you!"

They thought and thought, with their chins on their hands.

Michael thought of school, and that one

day he would have to go there. But even that seemed funny today and he had to laugh.

Jane thought: "I shall be grown up in another fourteen years!" But that didn't sound sad at all but quite nice and rather funny. She could not help smiling at the thought of herself grown up, with long skirts and a handbag.

"There was my poor old Aunt Emily," thought Mr Wigg out loud. "She was run over by an omnibus. Sad. Very sad. Unbearably sad. Poor Aunt Emily. But they saved her umbrella. That was funny, wasn't it?" And before he knew where he was, he was heaving and trembling and bursting with laughter at the thought of Aunt Emily's umbrella.

"It's no good," he said, blowing his nose. "I give it up. And my young friends here seem to be no better at sadness than I am. Mary, can't *you* do something? We want our tea."

To this day Jane and Michael cannot be sure of what happened then. All they know for certain is that, as soon as Mr Wigg had appealed to Mary Poppins, the table below began to wriggle on its legs. Presently it was swaying dangerously, and then with a rattle of china and with cakes lurching off their plates on to the cloth, the table came soaring through the room, gave one graceful turn, and landed beside them so that Mr Wigg was at its head.

"Good girl!" said Mr Wigg, smiling proudly upon her. "I knew you'd fix something. Now, will you take the foot of the table and pour out, Mary? And the guests on either side of me. That's the idea," he said, as Michael ran bobbing through the air and sat down on Mr Wigg's right. Jane was at his left hand. There they were, all together, up in the air and the table between them. Not a single piece of bread and butter or a lump of sugar had been left behind.

Mr Wigg smiled contentedly.

"It is usual, I think, to begin with bread and butter," he said to Jane and Michael, "but as it's my birthday we will begin the wrong way – which I always think is the *right* way – with the Cake!"

And he cut a large slice for everybody.

"More tea?" he said to Jane. But before she

had time to reply there was a quick, sharp knock at the door.

"Come in!" called Mr Wigg.

The door opened, and there stood Miss Persimmon with a jug of hot water on a tray.

"I thought, Mr Wigg," she began, looking searchingly round the room, "you'd be wanting some more hot— Well, I never! I simply *never*!" she said, as she caught sight of them all seated on the air round the table. "Such goings on I never did see! In all my born days

I never saw such. I'm sure, Mr Wigg, I always knew *you* were a bit odd. But I've closed my eyes to it – being as how you paid your rent regular. But such behaviour as this – having tea in the air with your guests – Mr Wigg, sir, I'm astonished at you! It's that undignified, and for a gentleman of your age – I never did—"

"But perhaps you will, Miss Persimmon!" said Michael.

"Will what?" said Miss Persimmon haughtily.

"Catch the Laughing Gas, as we did," said Michael.

Miss Persimmon flung back her head scornfully.

"I hope, young man," she retorted, "I have more respect for myself than to go bouncing about in the air like a rubber ball on the end of a bat. I'll stay on my own feet, thank you, or my name's not Amy Persimmon, and – oh dear, oh *dear*, my goodness, oh DEAR – what *is* the matter? I can't walk, I'm going, I – oh, help, HELP!"

For Miss Persimmon, quite against her

will, was off the ground and was stumbling
through the air, rolling from side to side like
a very thin barrel, balancing the tray in her
hand. She was almost weeping with distress
as she arrived at the table and put down her
jug of hot water.

"Thank you," said Mary Poppins in a calm,
very polite voice.

Then Miss Persimmon turned and went
wafting down again, murmuring as she went:
"So undignified – and me a well-behaved,
steady-going woman. I must see a doctor—"

When she touched the floor she ran hurriedly out of the room, wringing her hands,
and not giving a single glance backwards.

"So undignified!" they heard her moaning
as she shut the door behind her.

"Her name can't be Amy Persimmon,
because she *didn't* stay on her own feet!"
whispered Jane to Michael.

But Mr Wigg was looking at Mary Poppins
– a curious look, half-amused, half-accusing.

"Mary, Mary, you shouldn't – bless my soul,
you shouldn't, Mary. The poor old body will
never get over it. But, oh, my goodness, didn't

she look funny waddling through the air – my Gracious Goodness, but didn't she?"

And he and Jane and Michael were off again, rolling about the air, clutching their sides and gasping with laughter at the thought of how funny Miss Persimmon had looked.

"Oh dear!" said Michael. "Don't make me laugh any more. I can't stand it. I shall break!" "Oh, oh, oh!" cried Jane, as she gasped for breath, with her hand over her heart. "Oh, my Gracious, Glorious, Galumphing Goodness!" roared Mr Wigg, dabbing his eyes with his coat-tail because he couldn't find his handkerchief.

"IT IS TIME TO GO HOME." Mary Poppins' voice sounded above the roars of laughter like a trumpet.

And suddenly, with a rush, Jane and Michael and Mr Wigg came down. They landed on the floor with a huge bump, all together. The thought that they would have to go home was the first sad thought of the afternoon, and the moment it was in their minds the Laughing Gas went out of them.

Jane and Michael sighed as they watched Mary Poppins came slowly down the air, carrying Jane's coat and hat.

Mr Wigg sighed, too. A great, long, heavy sigh.

"Well, isn't that a pity?" he said soberly. "It's very sad that you've got to go home. I never enjoyed an afternoon so much – did you?"

"Never," said Michael sadly, feeling how dull it was to be down on the earth again with no Laughing Gas inside him.

"Never, never," said Jane, as she stood on tiptoe and kissed Mr Wigg's withered-apple cheeks. "Never, never, never, never . . . !"

They sat on either side of Mary Poppins going home in the bus. They were both very quiet, thinking over the lovely afternoon. Presently Michael said sleepily to Mary Poppins: "How often does your uncle get like that?"

"Like what?" said Mary Poppins sharply, as though Michael had deliberately said something to offend her.

"Well – all bouncy and boundy and laughing and going up in the air."

"Up in the air?" Mary Poppins' voice was high and angry. "What do you mean, pray, up in the air?" Jane tried to explain.

"Michael means – is your Uncle often full of Laughing Gas, and does he often go rolling and bobbing about in the ceiling when—"

"Rolling and bobbing! What an idea! Rolling and bobbing on the ceiling! You'll be telling me next he's a balloon!" Mary Poppins gave an offended sniff.

"But he did!" said Michael. "We saw him."

"What, roll and bob? How dare you! I'll have you know that my uncle is a sober, honest, hard-working man, and you'll be kind enough to speak of him respectfully. And don't bite your bus ticket! Roll and bob, indeed – the idea!"

Michael and Jane looked across Mary Poppins at each other. They said nothing, for they had learnt that it was better not to argue with Mary Poppins, no matter how odd anything seemed.

But the look that passed between them said: "Is it true or isn't it? About Mr Wigg. Is Mary Poppins right or are we?"

But there was nobody to give them the right answer.

The bus roared on, wildly lurching and bounding.

Mary Poppins sat between them, offended and silent, and presently, because they were very tired, they crept closer to her and leant up against her sides and fell asleep, still wondering . . .

Grimble's Monday

Clement Freud

This is a story about a boy called Grimble who was about ten. You may think it is silly to say someone is *about* ten, but Grimble had rather odd parents who were very vague and seldom got anything completely right.

For instance, he did not have his birthday on a fixed day like other children: every now and then his father and mother would buy a cake, put some candles on top of it, and say, "Congratulations Grimble. Today you are about seven", or, "Yesterday you were about eight and a half but the cake shop was closed." Of course there were disadvantages to having parents like that – like being called Grimble which made everyone say, "What is your real name?" and he had to say, "My real name is Grimble."

Grimble's father was something to do with going away, and his mother was a housewife by profession who liked to be with her husband whenever possible. Grimble went to school. Usually, when he left home in the morning, his parents were still asleep and there would be a note at the bottom of the stairs saying, *Enclosed please find ten p. for your breakfast.* As 10p is not very nourishing he used to take the money to a shop and get a glass of ginger beer, some broken pieces of meringue and a slice of streaky bacon. And at school he got lunch; that was the orderly part of his life. Shepherd's pie or sausages and mashed potatoes on Monday, Tuesday, Wednesday, Thursday; and on Fridays, fish fingers. This was followed by chocolate spodge – which is a mixture between chocolate sponge and chocolate sludge, and does not taste of anything very much except custard – which the school cook poured over everything.

*

One Monday Grimble came back from school, opened the door and shouted, "I am home." No one shouted anything in answer. So he went round the house looking for messages because his parents always left messages. It was the one thing they were really good at.

On a table in the sitting room there was a globe. And stuck into the globe were two pins, each with a triangle of paper on it. One of these was stuck into England and said *Grimble*, and the other was stuck into Peru and said *us*. He went into the kitchen and here was another note: *Tea is in the fridge, sandwiches in the oven. Have a good time.*

In the bedroom was a note saying *You will do your homework, won't you? P.S. don't forget to say your prayers.*

In the bathroom a message *Teeth.*

He walked round the house thinking they've really been very good, and then he went to the back-door and saw a note: *Milkman. No milk for five days.*

He changed the note to *Not much* milk for five days, and sat down in the kitchen and started to think about things. Five days is a long time for anyone and an especially long time for a boy of ten who is never quite sure whether he might not be missing his birthday. It had been weeks since he last had a birthday. He got a piece of paper and worked out five days at twenty-four hours a day and made it over a hundred hours, actually a hundred and something hours. He decided to have a sandwich. He opened the oven door, found the oven absolutely full of sandwiches, and took one with corned beef and apricot jam in it. It was a bit stale, like sandwiches are when they have been made a long time ago, so he lit the oven to freshen the sandwiches up a bit and decided to write a poem about his situation. This is what he wrote:

My Situation
by Grimble
When parents go to Peru
And leave cups of tea in the fridge,
It's jolly hard to know what to do
And I wish I could think of a useful
    word ending in idge.
The End

It was not a very good poem and it hadn't even taken very long to write, so he opened the door of the refrigerator and found bottles and bottles of tea. He poured himself a cup and sipped it. The tea did not taste very nice and it was not very hot, so he took his football out into the yard and kicked penalties with his left foot. As a matter of fact Grimble could not kick the ball at all with his right foot, but very few people knew this, so when he had friends whom he wanted to impress he used to say, "Come and see me kick penalties with my left foot." It worked very well.

After scoring one hundred and seven goals he went back to get a proper fresh sandwich. He opened the oven door and a very sad sight met his eyes. The sandwiches had been wrapped in pieces of paper, and the oven had burnt the paper, and all the butter had run out on to the bottom shelf, and the fillings of sandwich-spread and peanut butter and honey and lemon curd and cheese and pickles were sizzling in the butter. He got a teaspoon, tasted some of the mixture, and decided he preferred Weetabix, but as he was tasting it his eyes fell upon another note stuck onto the oven door and only a little bit brown from the heat of the roast sandwiches.

In case of emergency said the note *Go to* and there followed a list of five names and addresses all of them very near Grimble's house. He felt much better, kicked two more goals and went off to the house of the first name on the list.

Mr Wilfred Mosquito 29 Back Street (Ring Twice).

Back Street was just round the corner from his house, so he ran over there, and on the front door he found a note which said *Welcome Grimble, the key is in the milk bottle.* He opened the door, went in and found another note: *Food is in the kitchen. Kitchen is behind door marked kitchen*, and in the kitchen there was a big piece of paper which said: *Help yourself.*

The Mosquitoes' kitchen was big and bright, and there was a vegetable rack with coconuts and bananas and limes in it – limes are like lemons, only green – and a bottle of rum stood on the shelf, and the fridge had a lot of meat in it, all raw. He tried a sip of rum and did not like it much. It was strong. So he ate a banana and tried to kick a left-footed penalty with a coconut against the kitchen door, but a big chip of paint came off and he thought, I am a guest and I am not even supposed to chip paint off the doors in my own house; so he stuck the paint back on to the door again using the sludge on the inside of the banana skin as sticky paste, and went on an exploration of the house.

As far as he could see the Mosquitoes were a man and a woman and one child with a lot of clothes (or possibly three children with not very many clothes each), also six cats. He was sure about the six cats because he found them in a basket under the stairs. They had a saucer of milk and another saucer of meat that smelt a bit of fish. There were a lot of photographs of people in the sitting room and all the people in them were black. There was also a map of Jamaica. Grimble, who did not like to jump to conclusions but when it came to being a detective was every bit as good as Old Sexton B. and Sherlock H.

and Dixon of Dock G., decided that the Mosquitoes were Jamaicans.

He decided this especially when he found a newspaper called the *Daily Gleaner*, printed in Kingston, Jamaica. Reading the paper he noticed on the front page a message telling you to turn to page seven for this week's recipe, *Coconut Tart*.

He turned to page seven.

Coconut tart, wrote the good woman who had thought of the recipe, *can be made by a child of eight*.

As Grimble was older than eight he realized that he would be able to achieve a coconut tart with great ease, took the *Daily Gleaner* into the kitchen, propped it up against the coconut, and started to read the instructions.

Make a short pastry in the usual way, it began. Grimble thought this an exceedingly stupid remark and was pleased to see that the writer must have realized this also because she continued, *by taking half a pound of flour, quarter of a pound of fat, half a teaspoon of salt and two tablespoons of water. Or you can use one of those ready-made tart-cases.* "Why didn't you say so at the beginning, you stupid book!" said Grimble, and went out into the Mosquitoes' garden to try and catch a fat pigeon. The fourth time he threw his jacket over the fat pigeon's head, it gave him a sad tired look, waddled off and flew away.

Grimble went back into the kitchen.

For the filling, said the recipe in the paper, *you will need half a pound of grated coconut, a tablespoon of warm golden syrup, and two beaten eggs.*

He beat two eggs, and started to look for the coconut. It had gone. He remembered seeing it in the vegetable rack; he remembered kicking it, he remembered that very well because he still had a pain in his left foot. He read several pages of the *Daily Gleaner* to see if perhaps they said how one could make a coconut tart without a coconut, but all he found were pages and pages of small print headed *Work Wanted* and *Cars for Sale*, and it was not until he got to the last page that he found the coconut. It was propping up the paper.

Grimble like most small boys thought that a coconut grew on a piece of metal in the fairground, and did not know how one turned the hard brown hairy thing that never moved when you threw wooden balls at it into fluffy white coconut meat that you got in a chocolate coconut bar. He might never have found out if he had not decided to have one more left-footed penalty, using the kitchen table as the goal. The coconut hit the goalpost (actually the leg of the table), and broke in half. As it did so, a large puddle of white coconut milk seeped across the kitchen floor.

This was quite a helpful thing to happen. First of all it showed him where the fluffy white meat was, and secondly he had begun to feel he ought to do something about the six cats under the stairs, and now there was all this milk. He decided that six cats was much easier than a cloth and a bucket.

Grating a coconut is not as easy as it looks because the flesh grows on the inside of the shell and it means wedging it off before you can get at it. Also the grater had a big notice

tied to it which read *Grimble, mind your fingers,* so it was a slow business. But in the end it all worked, and he put the egg and syrup and coconut into the tart-case, and baked it the way they said, and shooed the cats out of the kitchen, and when the tart was cooked he ate it almost immediately. It was the best thing he had eaten since the corned beef and apricot jam sandwich.

When he had finished it was seven-fifteen, and as his official bed-time was seven-thirty, he went home. When he opened the door he saw a telegram on the mat. It was addressed to him. He opened it carefully and read the message: *Sending telegram tomorrow. Love Father and Mother.*

Just before he went to bed he wondered why they had not sent the message they were going to send tomorrow in today's telegram, but he got so mixed up trying to work it out that he brushed his teeth, said his prayers and fell asleep.

Burnt Offering

Anthony Buckeridge

Nothing ever seems to go quite according to plan for Jennings and his friend Darbishire, boarders at Linbury Court School. First there's the matter of Jennings' Victorian coin, stolen by horrible Mr Pink; and then there's Darbishire's hopeless attempt to buy a float and hook for their bargain fishing rod. Not to mention the nasty brush with the chap who looks exactly like Mr Pemberton-Oakes, their headmaster. And now even more trouble is in store. . .

Jennings learned a great deal about his coins from the book which Mr Carter had found for him in the county library. And the more he learned, the more angry he felt about the conduct of the perfidious Mr Pink. Quite apart from the financial loss, the missing half-sovereign had been an essential link in the range of Victorian coins which his Uncle Arthur had given him: without it, the set was incomplete.

He learned something, too, of the history of coins and the vocabulary of numismatics: he spoke knowingly of mint marks, coin clipping and intrinsic values.

"You shouldn't really talk about heads and tails," he informed everyone within ear shot at breakfast on Saturday morning. "The proper thing to say is obverse and reverse."

"Let's try it out, then," suggested Atkinson, scraping hopefully round the bottom of an empty jar of marmalade. "We could call *obs* or *revs* instead of heads or tails when we're tossing for choice of ends at football."

"Obs, I win – revs, you lose," said Temple from across the table. It was nearly the end of the meal and he was gathering up crusts and breadcrumbs from neighbouring plates and wrapping them in his handkerchief.

"Food parcel for the birds, sir," he

explained for the benefit of Mr Wilkins, who was watching his antics with distaste from the masters' table. "I've been feeding them every day this week since the weather got cold."

"Yes, I dare say, but why not put the scraps on a plate," Mr Wilkins retorted. "If I were a bird I should object to having my breakfast served up out of your revolting handkerchief. "It's enough to spoil a vulture's appetite!"

Temple grinned and transferred the offerings to his side plate. "Any more contributions?"

Atkinson gave him a bacon rind, and Venables donated a fragment of fried bread.

"That bit's for my favourite chaffinch, with my compliments, so don't let those greedy starlings have it," Venables commanded.

"It's first come, first served. Starlings get just as hungry as chaffinches: it's not fair to favour one lot against another," said the organizer of the feast.

During the winter months, feeding the birds was a popular (though somewhat haphazard) pastime which tended to tail off when the weather was mild and to revive again during cold spells. At such times, one of two boys would take on the daily task of collecting edible remains from their neighbours' plates for distribution to the birds foraging for food in the chilly world outside the dining-hall windows.

"If anybody wants the job they can have it," Temple declared. "I reckon I've done my bit. High time somebody else had a go.

Jennings at once accepted the offer. He and Darbishire could do it together, he decided. Before breakfast that morning they had agreed to postpone their fishing expedition until they had been able to acquire the final items of their equipment, and this new venture would absorb the time and energy which they would otherwise have spent in planning their angling activities.

So, for the best part of a week, Jennings and Darbishire took charge of the birds' breakfast and carried out their duties with zeal and efficiency.

With Jennings in charge, the catering became more varied in quality, more lavish in quantity: for, not satisfied with the meagre remains of Form Three's breakfasts, he collected scraps from farther afield and scavenged neighbouring tables in search of provender.

The birds were delighted and ate up every crumb of the fare provided. But on the following Friday an unfortunate incident occurred which not only put an end to the boys' feeding activities, but also obliged them to postpone their fishing expedition for a further two weeks.

The trouble started with an accident in the school kitchen while breakfast was being prepared. The menu was porridge followed by baked beans on toast, but five minutes before the breakfast bell rang, a strong smell of burning came wafting out from the kitchen, and drifts of smoke floated through the door, trailing along the corridor like a procession of thin, grey ghosts.

Inside the kitchen, Mrs Hackett could be seen enveloped in fog, coughing and spluttering with eyes streaming, trying to find a space to set down an enormous saucepan from which more foggy grey ghosts were escaping to freedom. By the time she had found somewhere to put it, two more saucepans were smouldering like volcanoes on the point of eruption.

It would not be fair to blame Mrs Hackett for the disaster, for she did not profess to be a cook. Normally, her duties at that hour of the day were confined to laying the tables and complaining that the dishwasher had gone wrong again. But that morning the housekeeper was in bed with a headache; and at the critical moment, just before the breakfast bell, the cook was outside in the yard talking to the milkman, the kitchen-helper was cutting the bread in the dining-hall, and only Mrs Hackett was available to keep an eye on the steaming porridge and the sizzling baked beans.

The accident occurred while she was in the pantry looking for a ladle. On her return, the kitchen was enveloped in smoke and fumes. It wasn't a dangerous situation, but it didn't improve the breakfast.

As a result, the meal that was served at

eight o'clock was barely edible and not at all appetising. A starving goat, desperate for food, might have had a good word to say for the burnt porridge and might not have criticised the blackened baked beans too harshly: but the Linbury boys, though hungry, were not as desperate as all that!

Most of them abandoned their porridge after the first spoonful, and laid down their forks after the first mouthful of little black bullets on charred hardboard into which the second course had disintegrated.

Fortunately, there was bread and butter and marmalade to follow; so, despite horrific warnings from Binns and Blotwell on the effects of famine and starvation, nobody actually collapsed from hunger during the course of the meal.

When breakfast was over, Jennings and Darbishire stayed behind in the dining-hall to gather up scraps for the birds: and that morning there was no shortage of scraps. Mrs Hackett had brought some waste buckets in from the kitchen and was scraping the plates so that they were fit to be stacked in the dishwasher.

"Lucky old birds! They won't have to tighten their belts today," said Jennings, as whole portions of porridge and beans slithered down into the buckets.

Darbishire looked at him in surprise. "You're not going to give them *all this*, are you?" he queried. "They're only supposed to have crumbs and crusts and things."

"Tut! How mean can you get! Don't be so stingy, Darbi," his friend replied, scathingly. "Here's our chance to give all the birds for miles around a really first-class, slap-up banquet, and you get all skinflinty and want to cut down their rations. I thought you *liked* birds!"

"So I do. I only meant – well, how d'you know they'll eat this sort of stuff? I couldn't touch it, myself."

"You're not a bird, are you!" came the logical answer. "Of course they'll eat it! Haven't you ever seen sparrows eating oats in a cornfield, or bullfinches belting into berries in a garden?"

"Yes, of course I have, but—"

"There you are, then; that proves it," the voice of reason went on. "The ones that like oats will eat the porridge, and the ones that like berries will eat the beans. And they all like toast because that's what we've been giving them nearly every morning."

Possibly true, probably not! Darbishire had his doubts. Changing his line of argument, he said, "Yes, but there's such a lot of it. They'd never eat it all."

Jennings led him to the window and pointed to the birds already gathering on the grass beyond the path. Sparrows, chaffinches, thrushes and blackbirds were hopping about expectantly, and blue tits and green finches were hovering in the branches above. A robin was perched on a rose bush and starlings were clustered on the path. In the middle distance six rooks and a crow, high in the trees, were keeping a wary eye on the scene, ready to swoop down when the time was ripe.

"Look at that lot, then!" said Jennings. "Hundreds of them sitting there like an audience waiting for the curtain to go up. You needn't worry about giving them too much:

there won't be a scrap left in half an hour from now."

Darbishire was convinced. On previous days the food had all disappeared in a matter of minutes, and today, with the weather even colder and the birds more numerous, it seemed pointless to consign the burnt offerings to the dustbins when their feathered friends were so obviously in want.

By now, Mrs Hackett had gone off to the scullery in search of more containers. So Darbishire threw open the window and Jennings picked up the waste buckets and emptied the remains of seventy-nine breakfasts on to the brick path outside. As a make-weight, he added four slices of unburnt toast which he found untouched on the masters' table.

"Perhaps we ought to spread it out a bit, so they can all get at it," Darbishire suggested as he shut the window, "We don't want the rooks keeping all the little ones off."

They went outside and found a thin branch of willow which had blown down in a recent gale. It made a useful broom, and with its aid

Jennings scattered the congealing sludge along the brickwork for a distance of twenty feet or so . . . The path was not a pretty sight by the time he had finished.

"I'm not sure we haven't overdone it a bit," Darbishire said, as the bell rang for morning assembly and they turned to go indoors.

"Don't worry, Darbi!" Jennings pointed to the feathered flock waiting to swoop down upon the feast. "Nobody's going to come along here before break, and it'll all be eaten up by then."

They hurried through the side door, leaving it ajar behind them . . . This was unfortunate, for a few moments later matron's cat, George III, slipped out to sniff the morning air.

George III was a well-built, agile, marmalade-coloured tom whose prowess at catching birds was well known to the feathered communities for miles around. At this hour of the morning he was usually to be found snoozing in front of the gas fire in Matron's dispensary, but on this occasion he decided to take a leisurely prowl round the grounds to see what mischief he could get up to.

The cat made his way along the brick path outside the dining-hall; and at his approach there was a flurry of wings, and the birds took flight, squawking out cries of warning. Sparrows, finches, thrushes and blackbirds sought refuge in the highest branches. Startled starlings and terrified tits took shelter amongst the chimney pots, and the rooks flapped away in a panic in search of a safer feeding-ground . . . There wasn't a bird in sight by the time the cat had reached the abandoned banquet.

George III sniffed the food and drew back with disdain, as though implying that no self-respecting cat would deign to sample such an unappetizing mess.

He wasn't going to let the birds have it, though! No fear! He settled down on the grass nearby and started to wash his whiskers in a leisurely manner.

Meanwhile, unaware of this disruption of their plan, Jennings and Darbishire made their way along to the Assembly Hall. As they waited for the headmaster's entrance, Jennings said, "I've been thinking about our fishing trip, Darbi. It's no good putting it off any longer just because we haven't got one or two bits and pieces. We'll have to make do with what we *have* got."

Darbishire pulled a face. "Fat lot of fish we'll catch if we haven't got a hook on the end of the line." He grinned. "And if we haven't got a float either, we'll have to train the fish to give a little tug when they're ready to be pulled up."

"Don't be funny," Jennings said reprovingly. "We'll just have to use home-made equipment, that's all. We could make a hook out of a safety pin, couldn't we!"

"M'yes, I suppose we could, but—"

"And for a float we could tie a cork on to the line. It'd do the job all right."

The suggestion sounded feasible. Darbishire scratched his nose thoughtfully. "Pity you didn't think of that before you sent me off on that dangerous mission all round Dunhambury, nearly running into the Head and all that."

"You didn't *nearly* run into him. You told me he wasn't even there."

"Ah, but at the time I thought—"

"Don't quibble, Darbi," Jennings broke in impatiently. "You said yourself that there weren't any fishing tackle shops in Dunhambury, so either we've got to make do with anything we can got hold of, or call the whole thing off."

It seemed the only answer, so in whispered tones, as they waited, they made their plans and decided to set out on the first of their angling expeditions the following Sunday afternoon.

But it was not to be!

The headmaster was late in arriving in the hall that morning, having been detained on the telephone by a visitor who was anxious to see the school. After assembly, while the boys were dispersing to their classrooms, Mr Pemberton-Oakes had a word with Mr Wilkins.

"I wonder if you'd mind keeping an eye on Five B during second period this morning, he said. "I'll set them some work, but I shan't be able to get along to their classroom, as I have a couple of prospective parents coming to see me."

Mr Wilkins nodded. "You'll be showing them round, I suppose?"

"Yes, of course. The husband said on the phone, just now, that they were most anxious to see the school at work. He sounded a somewhat – ah – pernickety sort of man – rather difficult to please, I should imagine, so I'm hoping everything will be in apple-pie order for their visit."

George III was still mounting guard over the congealed sludge outside the dining-hall windows an hour later as Mr Pemberton-Oakes was showing his guests round the school.

The visit was not proceeding smoothly . . . Form Five B had taken advantage of Mr Pemberton-Oakes' absence from their Latin lesson to stage a medieval jousting tournament between the desks. They scurried to their places when the headmaster opened the door but, even so, it was too late to prevent a badly-aimed blackboard duster from striking the lintel above the doorway and showering the visitors with a spray of chalk-dust as they stood on the threshold. As the duster dropped down, it caught Mr Pemberton-Oakes a glancing blow on the right shoulder.

After that, the visitors were shown the Art Room, arriving at the very moment that Blotwell accidentally dropped a tray containing six jars of poster paint, spattering the boys around him in rainbow hues of red, orange, yellow, green, blue and mauve.

Mr Pemberton-Oakes was tight-lipped with embarrassment as he led his visitors out through the side door on the next stage of their conducted tour. As he had feared, the prospective parents had turned out to be pernickety in the extreme, and it was clear from the look on their faces that from what they had seen so far of Linbury Court School, they didn't think much of it.

The headmaster did his best to make light of the unfortunate incidents as his guests followed him out-of-doors.

"The dining-hall is along here in the new

block," he was saying as they headed towards the brick path. "Our catering at Linbury is first-rate. We make a point of seeing that the boys always start the day with a wholesome and appetizing breakfast."

So saying, he turned the corner and walked straight into the remains of seventy-nine wholesome and appetizing breakfasts spread out along the path in congealed and unsightly clumps.

They were all in it up to the ankles before

they could check their pace. Porridge and beans lapped the welts of their shoes: blackened cinders of fried bread crunched and slithered underfoot.

The headmaster was speechless with mortification as his guests squelched their way out of the morass.

"Perhaps we should retrace our steps," he began diffidently when speech returned; but the damage was irretrievable.

"Thank you, but we have seen enough." The husband turned to his wife. "I think we had better be going. We have another school to see this morning."

In silence, Mr Pemberton-Oakes escorted them to their car, conscious, as he walked, of the piece of toast still impaled on the heel of his shoe.

The parting was polite, but not cordial: it would be stretching the facts to claim that the prospective parents had been impressed by their visit to Linbury Court.

Who's the Lucky Bride?

Judy Blume

There are two people in Pete's life who drive him crazy. The first is his infuriating little brother, Fudge. The second is Sheila Tubman who lives in the same apartment block. Somehow, wherever Pete goes, Sheila manages to be there too . . .

"**G**uess what, Pete?" my brother, Fudge, said. "I'm getting married tomorrow."

I looked up from my baseball cards. "Isn't this kind of sudden?" I asked, since Fudge is only five.

"No," he said.

"Well . . who's the lucky bride?"

"Sheila Tubman," Fudge said.

I hit the floor, pretending to have fainted dead away. I did a good job of it because Fudge started shaking me and shouting, "Get up, Pete!"

What's with this Pete *business*? I thought. *Ever since he could talk, he's called me* Pee-tah.

Then Tootsie, my sister, who's just a year and a half, danced around me singing, "Up, Pee . . . up."

Next, Mom was beside me saying, "Peter . . . what happened? Are you all right?"

"I told him I was getting married," Fudge said. "And he just fell over."

"I fell over when you told me *who* you were marrying," I said.

"Who are you marrying, Fudge?" Mom asked, as if we were seriously discussing his wedding.

"Sheila Tubman," Fudge said.

"Don't say that name around me," I told him, "or I'll faint again."

"Speaking of Sheila Tubman . . ." Mom began.

But I didn't wait for her to finish. "You're making me feel very sick . . ." I warned.

"Really, Peter . . ." Mom said. "Aren't you over doing it?"

I clutched my stomach and moaned but Mom went right on talking. "Buzz Tubman is the one who told us about the house in Maine."

"*M-a-i-n-e* spells *Maine*," Fudge sang.

Mom looked at him but didn't even pause. "And this house is right next to the place they've rented for their vacation," she told me.

"I'm missing something here," I said. "What house? What vacation?"

"Remember we decided to go away for a few weeks in August?"

"Yeah . . . so?"

"So we got a great deal on a house in Maine."

"And the Tubmans are going to be next door?" I couldn't believe this. "Sheila Tubman . . . next door . . . for two whole weeks?"

"Three," Mom said.

I fell back flat on the floor.

"He did it again, Mom!" Fudge said.

"He's just pretending," Mom told Fudge. "He's just being very silly."

"So I don't have to marry Sheila tomorrow," Fudge said. "I'll marry her in Maine."

"That makes more sense," Mom said. "In Maine you can have a nice wedding under the trees."

"Under the trees," Fudge said.

"Tees . . ." Tootsie said, throwing a handful of Gummi Bears in my face.

And that's how it all began.

That night we went to Tico-Taco for supper. I wasn't very hungry. The idea of spending three weeks next door to Sheila Tubman was enough to take away my appetite. I wish the Tubmans would move to another planet! But until that happens there's no way to avoid Sheila. She lives in our apartment building. We go to the same school.

I kind of groaned and Dad looked at me. "What is it, Peter?"

"Sheila Tubman," I said.

"What about her?" Dad asked.

"We're getting married," Fudge said, his mouth full of chicken and taco shell.

"I'm not talking about your wedding," I said. "I'm talking about spending three weeks in Maine next door to the Tubmans."

"It won't be as bad as you think," Mom said.

"You don't know how bad I *think* it will be!"

"Sheila's older now. She's finished sixth grade, same as you."

"What's age got to do with it?" I said. "She'll still be the Queen of Cooties."

"What's *cooties*?" Fudge asked.

When I didn't answer he tugged on my sleeve.

"What's *cooties*, Pete?"

"Since when am I *Pete*?" I asked, shaking him off.

"Since today," he said.

"Well, I prefer Peter, if you don't mind."

"Pete is a better name for a big brother."

"And Farley is a better name for a little brother!"

I figured that would shut him up since his real name is Farley Drexel Hatcher and he's ready to kill anybody who calls him that.

"Don't call me Farley!" he said. Then he really let go and yelled, "I'm *Fudge*!"

The waiter, who heard him from across the room, came over to our table and said, "Sorry . . . we don't have any tonight. But we do have mud pie, which is almost the same thing."

Dad had to explain that we weren't talking about dessert. And Mom added, "We never eat dessert until we've finished our main course."

"Oh," the waiter said.

But before he had a chance to get away, Fudge looked up at him and said, "Do you have cooties?"

"Cooties?" the waiter asked. "For dessert?" He looked confused. Especially when Tootsie banged her spoon against the tray of her baby seat and sang, "Coo-tee . . . coo-tee . . ."

I could tell Fudge was about to ask the same question *again*, but before he had the chance I clamped my hand over his mouth. Then Dad told the waiter we didn't need anything else right now.

The waiter walked away shaking his head

and I took my hand away from Fudge's mouth. As soon as I did, he was back in business. "What's *cooties*?" This time the people at the next table looked over at us.

"They're like nits," Mom told him quietly.

"What's *nits*?" Fudge asked

"Head lice," Dad said, almost in a whisper.

"Head mice?" Fudge asked.

"Not mice, Turkey Brain," I told him. "*Lice*. Little creepy, crawly bugs that live in hair." I snapped my fingernails at his head the way Sheila Tubman used to do to me.

Fudge yelled, "I don't want creepy, crawly bugs in my hair!"

Now everyone in the restaurant looked over at us.

"That's enough, Peter," Dad said.

"Well, he's the one who wanted to know."

"That's *enough*," Mom said. It came out sounding like *eee-nuff*, which got Tootsie going.

"Eee-eee-eee-eee..." Tootsie shrieked, banging her spoon.

This is the way it's going to be all summer, I thought, *only worse*. So I put down my taco and said, "Maybe I should go to camp in August."

Dad got this really serious look on his face. "We don't have the money this year, Peter. We wouldn't be going away at all if it weren't for Grandma, who's paying more than her share."

"But if you want, you can bring a friend," Mom said.

"A friend?" I asked. "You mean like Jimmy Fargo?" They both nodded.

Jimmy is my best friend in New York. We've always wanted to spend the summer together.

"What about me?" Fudge asked. "Can I bring a friend, too?"

I held my breath.

"You'll find a friend in Maine," Mom told him.

"Suppose I don't?" Fudge asked.

"You're getting married," I reminded him.

"Does that mean I don't get a friend?" Fudge asked.

"Of course not," Mom told him. "I'm married and I have friends. Daddy's married and he has friends."

"What about Uncle Feather?" I said. Uncle

Feather is Fudge's mynah bird. "He's your friend, isn't he?"

"I can't play with Uncle Feather," Fudge said. "He's not that kind of friend. And I can't marry him either. If he was a girl bird it would be different."

"People don't marry birds," I told him.

"Some people do."

"Name one," I said.

"The guy who's married to Big Bird on *Sesame Street.*

"Big Bird's not married," I said.

"That's how much you know!" Fudge shouted.

He's learned to say that every time someone disagrees with him. It's a real conversation stopper.

"I give up!" I said, going back to my taco, which was getting soggy.

"Up," Tootsie repeated, holding her arms. "Up . . . up . . . up."

Dad lifted her out of the baby seat and she squirmed until he put her down. Then she took off, toddling through the restaurant, stopping at every table. Fudge scrambled off his chair and ran after her. Eating out with my family is not exactly relaxing.

"Here, girl . . ." Fudge said, as if he were calling a dog. "Here's something just for you." He lured her back to our table and dropped some of his taco on her tray. "Yum . . ." he said to her. "Yum . . . yum . . . yum . . ."

Dad put Tootsie back into her seat. She stuffed the chicken pieces into her mouth.

"I always know what Tootsie wants," Fudge said. "That's why I'm her favourite brother."

"Tootsie doesn't have favourites," Mom told him. "She loves both her brothers."

"But she loves me best!" Fudge said. Then he looked at me and laughed. When he did, half the food in his mouth wound up on my shirt.

I called Jimmy Fargo as soon as we got home. I asked him to come to Maine with us.

"Three weeks next door to Sheila Tubman?"

"The houses are really far apart," I said. Nobody told me this but I was hoping it was true. "You won't even be able to see her house. There'll probably be a forest separating us."

When he didn't say anything I added, "And don't forget . . . Sheila's scared of dogs so we can get Turtle after her any time she tries to give us trouble." Turtle is my dog. He's big enough to look scary but he'd never hurt anybody. Lucky for us, Sheila doesn't know that.

Jimmy laughed. "Maybe I can come for a week."

"A week isn't long enough!"

"Hey, Peter . . . no offence . . . but a week with your family can feel like a long time."

That's because Jimmy's the only kid in his family. His parents are divorced. He lives with his father, Frank Fargo, who's a painter.

"How about two weeks?" I said.

"Is your brother bringing his bird?"

"Yeah . . . Uncle Feather's part of the family," I told him. "Same as Turtle."

"So it will be your mother, your father, Fudge, Tootsie, Turtle, Uncle Feather and you?"

"Right," I said. "And my grandmother's coming too."

"The one who taught you to stand on your head?"

"Yeah." Grandma Muriel is Mom's mother. She ran a gymnastics camp before she retired.

"You think she could teach me?" Jimmy asked.

"Maybe," I said.

"I'll talk to my father," Jimmy said. "I'll let you know tomorrow."

He called back the next morning. Mr Fargo

liked the idea of Maine. He liked it so much he said he'd drive Jimmy up and camp out in the area himself.

"That's great!" I said. Maybe three weeks in Maine wouldn't be as bad as I'd thought.

It took ten hours to drive to Southwest Harbour, Maine. Ten hours in the back seat of an old Blazer with Fudge, Tootsie, Turtle and Uncle Feather, who wouldn't shut up. Some mynah birds don't talk at all but Uncle Feather's not one of them. He'll repeat anything you say. Finally, I dropped the cover over his cage, hoping he'd think it was nighttime. "Go to sleep, stupid!" I told him. *Stupid* is one of his favourite words.

But that didn't work either. "Go to sleep, stupid . . ." he chanted, until even Turtle lost patience and started barking. *Grandma is really smart*, I thought. *She's flying up to Maine.*

As we got closer to our destination, Mom started reading to us from a guidebook. "Southwest Harbour is on an island called Mount Desert." She pronounced it de-*sert*.

"Ice cream, cookies, brownies, pudding . . ." Fudge sang.

Mom kept right on reading. I don't know why she thinks Fudge pays any attention to her lectures on history. He hears only what he wants to hear. Everything else goes right by him.

"Founded in 1905, the town of Southwest Harbour . . ." *You call this a town?* I thought, as we drove through it. There was one street with a couple of shops. And that was about it. But I could tell Mom was really excited. She put down her guidebook and smiled at my father. "Oh, it's so quaint," she said. "Isn't it quaint, Warren?"

And my father smiled back and said, "It's perfect, honey."

Fudge chucked Tootsie under her chin. "It's perfect, honey," he said, imitating my father.

Then Uncle Feather started. "*Honey . . . honey . . . honey.*" For some reason Tootsie thought that was wildly funny, and she laughed until she got the hiccups. Mom passed a bottle of water to the back seat and

101

I stuck it in Tootsie's mouth.

"Take a left here, Warren," Mom said to Dad. We turned on to a dirt road, then pulled into a gravel driveway and parked in front of an old, weathered wood house. The first person I saw was the Queen of Cooties herself. She was standing on the seat of a rope swing. It hung from the branch of a big tree in the front yard.

She was swinging pretty high when I opened the back door of the Blazer and Turtle jumped out. It had been almost four hours since I'd walked him and he really had to go. He raced for the woods behind the house but Sheila thought he was heading straight for her.

"Help!" she screamed, wobbling on the swing.

"Somebody please heeelp!" She lost her balance and fell to the ground. *What a dork*!

Mom jumped out of the car and ran to her rescue. "It's all right," she said, helping Sheila to her feet.

"Turtle just had to wee-wee." How could

Mom have used such an embarrassing expression?

By then Mr and Mrs Tubman, who had also heard Sheila's screams, came running out of the house. "Are you okay?" Mrs Tubman asked Sheila.

"I'm fine," Sheila said brushing herself off. "It was just that *disgusting* dog!"

Before I had the chance to tell her who was *really* disgusting, a man with white hair called, "Lemonade . . ." We all headed for the house and gathered around the table on the porch. "I'm Buzz Tubman's father," the white-haired man said. He poured each of us a glass of lemonade. "Call me Buzzy Senior."

I polished off my drink really fast. Buzzy Senior poured me another. I gulped it down. "Long trip up here, isn't it?" he asked.

"Ten hours," I said, wiping my mouth with the back of my hand. He filled my glass again.

I didn't even notice Fudge watching until then. "You must be really thirsty, Pete."

"Yeah," I said.

"Remember that time you drank too much Island Punch and you . . ."

I clamped my hand over his mouth. He still doesn't get the difference between stories you tell to strangers and stories you keep to yourself. I looked at Buzzy Senior. "Fudge knows a lot about dinosaurs," I said, hoping to change the subject.

But as soon as I took my hand away from his mouth Fudge laughed. "And Pete knows all about cooties."

"Well, you can't know too much about cooties, can you, Pete?" Buzzy Senior said, smiling at me.

"And guess what else?" Fudge said. "I'm getting married under the trees."

"Do I know the bride?" Buzzy Senior asked.

"It's Sheila Tubman!" Fudge said.

"Oh, my granddaughter," Buzzy Senior said.

"Sheila's your granddaughter?" Fudge asked.

Buzzy Senior nodded. "Have you popped the question yet?"

"How do you *pop* a question?" Fudge said.

"You have to ask if she *wants* to marry you," Buzzy Senior explained.

"Why wouldn't she want to marry me?"

"It's something you have to decide together," Buzzy Senior said.

"Okay . . ." Fudge said. He turned towards Sheila, who was sitting in a rocking chair. "Hey, Sheila . . . you want to marry me . . . right?"

Sheila laughed so hard she nearly fell off the chair.

"See . . ." Fudge said. "I popped the question and she wants to marry me."

"Congratulations," Buzzy Senior said. "You're a lucky man."

Lucky? I thought. That's not what I'd call it.

The screen door opened and Libby stepped out on to the porch. Libby is Sheila's older sister. She's almost sixteen but no one would make the mistake of calling her *sweet*. She was carrying a small white-and-brown puppy.

Sheila jumped. I expected her to run for her life. Instead, she cooed, "Oooh . . . my baby . . . my precious furry baby . . ." She kissed the puppy about twenty times.

"You have a dog?" I asked.

"Yes," Sheila said proudly. "Her name is Jake and we just got her. Isn't she adorable?"

"I thought you're afraid of dogs."

"She is," Libby said.

"I'm *not* afraid of Jake!"

"She's afraid of dogs, in general," Libby told me.

"That is sooo unfair!" Sheila said.

"But it's true, isn't it?" Libby asked in her most obnoxious voice.

"I just don't like big, smelly, *disgusting* dogs," Sheila said, looking directly at me.

"Are you calling *my* dog smelly and disgusting?" I asked.

Sheila folded her arms and smiled. "Turtle is the *most* disgusting dog ever born!"

"You want to see disgusting . . . look in the mirror," I told her. "You want to smell disgusting . . . smell yourself!"

"Are you two going to argue for three weeks?" Libby asked. "Because that could get to be a real bore."

"You're right," I said. "So why don't you just tell me where *our* house is and that'll be the end of it."

"This *is* your house," Sheila said.

"I thought this was *your* house."

"It's *two* houses, but they're connected."

"What do you mean *connected*?" I asked.

"Didn't you learn anything in sixth grade, Peter? *Connected* means attached . . . joined together . . ."

"I *know* what the word means," I told her.

"Don't worry," Sheila said, "there's an inside door that separates your house from ours."

An inside door? I thought. *How am I going to explain this to Jimmy Fargo? I promised him a forest between our houses . . . not an inside door!*

Suddenly we heard a rustling sound and a minute later Turtle came tearing out of the woods. A terrible smell followed him. I mean *really* bad.

"Eeeuuuw . . ." Sheila cried, holding her nose. "Whath that thmell?

"Ith thkunk!" Dad said, holding his. "Turtle'th been thprayed by a thkunk."

"Oh no!" Mom said. She held her nose, too. "Not thkunk!"

They all sounded as if they had the worst colds. I would have laughed except for the smell. It was so strong I had to hold my nose, just like the rest of them.

"Thith ith too nautheating for wordth!" Libby said, grabbing Jake and running back into the house.

"Do thomething, Peter!" Sheila yelled.

"What am I thuppoth to do?"

"He'th *your* dog, ithn't he?"

"Leth not panic," Mr Tubman said. "Leth think thith through in a logical way."

"Thith ithn't the time for logic!" Mrs Tubman said. "Thith ith the time for action!"

"Tomato juith!" Buzzy Senior said. "Put him in a tub of tomato juith."

"Where am I thuppoth to get enough tomato juith to cover him?" Mrs Tubman asked.

"I'll take care of it, Jean!" Dad said. "Don't worry." He headed for the Blazer.

Fudge chased Dad. "Wait for me!"

"Where are you going, Warren?" Mom called.

"For tomato juith!" Dad called back.

All this time Turtle was rolling over and over in the grass, trying to get rid of the awful smell. He knew he was in big trouble.

"I alwayth knew your dog wath the thmellieth dog in the entire world," Sheila said. "And thith provth it!"

For once I had to agree.

Not Just a Witch

Eva Ibbotson

Miss H. Tenbury-Smith has moved to Wellbridge to live on her own and "do good". But being an "animal witch", she has some very interesting views on the relative merits of humans and animals . . .

It was a boy called Daniel who found out that a witch had come to live in Wellbridge.

He found out the night he went to baby-sit for Mr and Mrs Boothroyd at The Towers. Mr Boothroyd owned a factory on the edge of the town which made bath plugs and he was very rich. Unfortunately he was also very mean and so was his wife. As for his baby, which was called Basil, it was quite the most unpleasant baby you could imagine. Most babies have *something* about them which is all right. The ones that look like shrivelled chimpanzees often have nice fingernails; the ones that look like half-baked buns often smile very sweetly. But Basil was an out and out disaster. When Basil wasn't screaming he was kicking; when he wasn't kicking he was throwing up his food and when he wasn't doing that he was holding his breath and turning blue.

Daniel was really too young to baby-sit and so was Sumi who was his friend. But Sumi, whose parents had come over from India to run the grocery shop in the street behind Daniel's house, was so sensible and so used to minding her three little brothers that the Boothroyds knew she would be fit to look after Basil while they went to the Town Hall to have dinner with the Lord Mayor. What's more, they knew they would have to pay her much less than they would have to pay a grown-up for looking after their son.

And Sumi had suggested that Daniel came along. "I'll ask you your spellings," she said, because she knew how cross Daniel's parents got when he didn't do brilliantly at school.

Daniel's parents were professors. Both of them. His father was called Professor Trent and if only Daniel had been dead and buried in some interesting tomb somewhere, the Professor would have been delighted with him. He was an archaeologist who studied ancient tribes and in particular their burial customs and he was incredibly clever. But Daniel wasn't mummified or covered in clay so the Professor didn't have much time for him. Daniel's mother (who was also called Professor Trent) was a philosopher who had written no less than seven books on The Meaning of Meaning and she too was terribly clever and found it hard to understand that her son was just an ordinary boy who sometimes got his sums wrong and liked to play football.

The house they lived in was tall and grey and rather dismal, and looked out across the river to the university where both the professors worked, and to the zoo. As often as not when Daniel came home from school there was nobody there, just notes propped against the teapot telling him what to unfreeze for supper and not to forget to do his piano practice.

When you know you are a disappointment to your parents, your school-friends become very important. Fortunately Daniel had plenty of these. There was Joe whose father was a keeper in the Wellbridge Zoo, and Henry whose mother worked as a chambermaid in the Queen's Hotel. And there was Sumi who was so gentle and so clever and never showed off even though she knew the answers to everything. And because it was Sumi who asked him, he went along to babysit at The Towers.

The Boothroyds' house was across the river in a wide, tree-lined street between the university and the zoo. They had been quite old when Basil was born and they dressed him like babies were dressed years ago. Basil slept in a barred cot with a muslin canopy and blue bows; his pillow was edged with lace and he had a silken quilt. And there he sat, in a long white nightdress, steaming away like a red and angry boil.

The Boothroyds left. Sumi and Daniel settled down on the sitting room sofa. Sumi took out the list of spellings.

"Separate," she said, and Daniel sighed. He was not very fond of separate.

But it didn't matter because at that moment Basil began to scream.

He screamed as though he was being stuck all over with red-hot skewers and by the time they got upstairs he had turned an unpleasant shade of puce and was banging his head against the side of the cot.

Sumi managed to gather him up. Daniel ran to warm his bottle under the tap. Sumi gave it to him and he bit off the teat. Daniel ran to fetch another. Basil took a few windy gulps, then swivelled round and knocked the bottle out of Sumi's hand.

It took a quarter of an hour to clean up the mess and by the time they got downstairs again, Sumi had a long scratch across her cheek.

"Separate," she said wearily, picking up the list.

"S . . . E . . . P . . ." began Daniel – and was

wondering whether to try an A or an E when Basil began again.

This time he had been sick all over the pillow. Sumi fetched a clean pillow-case and Basil took a deep breath and filled his nappy. She managed to change him, kicking and struggling, and put on a fresh one. Basil waited till it was fastened, squinted – and filled it again.

It went on like this for the next hour. Sumi never lost her patience, but she was looking desperately tired and Daniel, who knew how early she got up each day to mind her little brothers and help tidy the shop before school, could gladly had murdered Basil Boothroyd.

At eight o'clock they gave up and left him. Basil went on screaming for a while and then – miracle of miracles – he fell silent. But when Daniel looked across at Sumi for another dose of spelling he saw that she was lying back against the sofa cushions. Her long dark hair streamed across her face and she was fast asleep.

Daniel should now have felt much better. Sumi was asleep, there was no need to spell separate and Basil was quiet. And for about ten minutes he did.

Then he began to worry. *Why* was Basil so quiet? Had he choked? Had he bitten his tongue out and bled to death?

Daniel waited a little longer. Then he crept upstairs and stood listening by the door.

Basil wasn't dead. He was snoring. Daniel was about to go downstairs again when something about the noise that Basil was making caught his attention. Basil was snoring, but he was snoring . . . nicely. Daniel couldn't think of any other way of putting it. It was a cosy, snuffling snore and it surprised Daniel because he didn't think that Basil could make any noise that wasn't horrid.

Daniel put his head round the door . . . took a few steps into the room.

And stopped dead.

At first he simply didn't believe it. What had happened was so amazing, so absolutely wonderful, that it couldn't be real. Only it *was* real. Daniel blinked and rubbed his eyes and shook himself, but it was still there, curled up on the silken quilt: not a

screaming, disagreeable baby, but the most
enchanting bulldog puppy with a flat,
wet nose, a furrowed forehead and a blob
of a tail.

Daniel stood looking down at it, feeling quite
light-headed with happiness, and the puppy
opened its eyes. They were the colour of
liquorice and brimming with soul. There are
people who say that dogs don't smile, but
people who say that are silly. The bulldog
grinned. It sat up and wagged its tail. It licked
Daniel's hands.

"Oh, I do so like you," said Daniel to the little, wrinkled dog.

And the dog liked Daniel. He lay on his back so that Daniel could scratch his stomach; he jumped up to try and lick Daniel's face, but his legs were too short and he collapsed again. Daniel had longed and longed for a dog to keep him company in that tall, grey house to which his parents came back so late. Now it seemed like a miracle, finding this funny, loving, squashed-looking little dog in place of that horrible baby.

Because Basil had gone. There was no doubt about it. He wasn't in the cot and he wasn't under it. He wasn't anywhere. Daniel searched the bathroom, the other bedrooms . . . Nothing. Someone must have come in and taken Basil and put the little dog there instead. A kidnapper? Someone wanting to hold Basil to ransom? But why leave the little dog? The Boothroyds might not be very bright, but they could tell the difference between their baby and a dog.

I must go and tell Sumi, he thought, and it was only then that he became frightened, seeing what was to come. The screaming parents, the police, the accusations. Perhaps they'd be sent to prison for not looking after Basil properly. And where *was* Basil? He might be an awful baby, but nobody wanted him harmed.

Daniel tore himself away from the bulldog and studied the room.

How could the kidnappers have got in? The front door was locked, so was the back and the window was bolted. He walked over to the fireplace. It was the old-fashioned kind with a wide chimney. But that was ridiculous – even if the kidnappers had managed to come down it, how could they have got the baby off the roof?

Then he caught sight of something spilled in the empty grate: a yellowish coarse powder, like breadcrumbs.

He scooped some up, felt it between his fingers, put it to his nose. Not breadcrumbs. Goldfish food. He knew because the only pet his parents had allowed him to keep was a goldfish he'd won in a fair, and it had died almost at once because of fungus on its fins. And he knew too where the goldfish food came from: the corner pet shop, two streets away from his house. The old man who kept it made it himself; it had red flecks in it and always smelled very odd.

Daniel stood there and his forehead was almost as wrinkled as the little dog's. For the pet shop had been sold a week ago to a queer-looking woman. Daniel had seen her moving about among the animals and talking to herself. She'd been quite alone, just the sort of woman who might snatch a baby to keep her company. He'd read about women like that taking babies from their prams while their mothers were inside a supermarket. The police usually caught them – they weren't so much evil as crazy.

Daniel gave the puppy a last pat and went downstairs. Sumi was still asleep, one hand trailing over the side of the sofa. For a moment he wondered whether to wake her. Then he let himself very quietly out of the house and began to run.

He ran across the bridge, turned into Park Avenue where his house was, then plunged into the maze of small streets that led between the river and the market place. Sumi's parents' shop was in one of these, and close by, on the corner, was the pet shop.

Daniel had been inside it often when the old man owned it, but now he stood in front of it, badly out of breath and very frightened. It was dusk, the street-lamps had just been lit and he could see the notice above the door.

Under new management, it said. *Proprietor; Miss H. Tenbury-Smith.*

There was no one downstairs; the blinds were drawn, but upstairs, he could see one lighted window.

Daniel put his hand up to ring the bell and dropped it again. His knees shook, his heart was pounding. Suddenly it seemed to him that he was quite mad coming here. If the woman in the shop had taken Basil, she was certainly not going to hand him over to a schoolboy. She was much more likely to kidnap him too or even murder him so that he couldn't tell the police.

He was just turning away, ready to run for it, when the door suddenly opened and a woman stood in the hallway. She was tall with frizzy hair and looked brisk and eager like a hockey mistress in an old-fashioned girl's school. And she was smiling!

"Come in, come in," said Miss Tenbury-Smith. "I've been expecting you."

Daniel stared at her. "But how . . ." he stammered. "I mean, I've come—"

"I know why you've come, dear boy. You've come to thank me. How people can say that children nowadays are not polite, I cannot understand. I expect you'd like some tea?"

Quite stunned by all this, Daniel followed her through the dark shop, with its rustlings and squeakings, and up a narrow flight of stairs. Miss Tenbury-Smith's flat was cosy. A gas fire hissed in the grate, there were pictures of middle-aged ladies in school blazers, and on the mantelpiece, a framed photograph with its face turned to the wall.

"Unless you'd rather have fruit juice?" she went on. And as Daniel continued to stare at her, "You're admiring my dressing-gown. It's pure batskin – a thousand bats went into its making. And in case you're wondering – *every single one of those bats died in its sleep.* I would never, never wear the skin of an animal that had not passed away peacefully from old age. Never!"

But now Daniel felt he had to get to the point. "Actually, it's about the Boothroyd baby that I've come," he said urgently.

"Well, of course it is, dear boy. What else?" said Miss Tenbury-Smith. "You're quite certain that tea would suit you?"

"Yes . . . tea would be fine. Only, please, Miss Tenbury-Smith, my friend is in such trouble. We're baby-sitting and the Boothroyds are due back any minute and there'll be such a row, so could you possibly give Basil back? Just this once?"

"Give him back? Give him *back*?" Her voice had risen to an outraged squeak.

"Well, you swopped him . . . didn't you? You kidnapped him?" But Daniel's voice trailed away, suddenly uncertain.

Miss Tenbury-Smith put down the teapot. Her slightly protruding eyes had turned stony. Her eyebrows rose. "I . . . *kidnapped* . . . Basil Boothroyd?" she repeated, stunned. Her long nose twitched and she looked very sad. "I was so sure we were going to be friends, Daniel," she said, and he looked up, amazed that she should know his name. "And now this!" She sighed. Now listen carefully. "When you have kidnapped somebody you have got him. You agree with that? He is with you. He is part of your life."

"Yes."

"And would you imagine that a person in their right mind would want to have Basil? Even for five minutes? Or are you suggesting that I am *not* in my right mind?"

"No . . . no . . . But—"

"I came to Wellbridge to Do Good, Daniel. It's my mission in life to make the world a better place." She tapped the side of her long nose. "It hurts, you know, to be misunderstood."

"So you didn't swop Basil for the little dog?"

"Swopped him? Of course I didn't swop him. Oh, I had so *hoped* that you would be my friend. I'm really very fond of boys with thin faces and big eyes. Some people would say

125

your ears are on the large side, but personally I like large ears. But I can't be doing with a friend who is stupid."

"I want to be your friend," said Daniel, who did indeed want it very much. "But I don't understand. You're . . . Are you . . .? Yes, of course; I see. You're a witch!"

Miss Tenbury-Smith began to pour out the tea, but she had forgotten the tea-bags.

"Well, I'm glad you see something," she said. "But the point is, I'm not just a witch; I'm a witch who means to make the world a better place. Now let me ask you a question. Have you ever seen a kangaroo throwing a bomb into a supermarket, killing little children?"

"No, I haven't."

"Good. Have you ever seen an anteater hijack an aeroplane?"

"No."

"Or a hamster go round knocking old ladies on the head and stealing their hand-bags? Have you ever seen a coshing hamster?"

"No."

"Exactly. It's very simple. Animals are not wicked. It is people who are wicked. So you might think wicked people should be killed."

"Yes . . . I suppose so."

"However, killing is bad. It is wicked. And I'm not a wicked witch, I'm a good witch. And I do good by turning wicked people into animals."

She leant back, pleased with herself, and took a sip of hot water.

Daniel stared at her. "You mean . . . you changed Basil into a dog? Into that lovely dog?"

"Yes, I did. I'm so glad you liked it. I adore bulldogs: the way they snuffle and snort, and those deep chests. When you take a bulldog on a ship, you have to face them upwind because their noses are so flat. It's the only way they can breathe. Of course, when I changed that dreadful baby, I was just limbering up. Wellbridge is a little damp, being so low-lying, and I wasn't sure how it would affect my Knuckle of Power." She stuck out her left hand and showed him a purple swelling on the joint. "If you get rheumatism on your knuckle it can make things very tricky. But it all went like a dream. I really did it for that pretty friend of yours – so polite, and such a nice shop her parents keep with everything higgledy-piggledy, not like those boring supermarkets. Poor children, I thought, they're going to have such a horrible evening."

"Yes, but you see it's going to be much more horrible if the Boothroyds come and find Basil gone. There'll be such trouble. So, please, could you change Basil back? If you can?"

"If I *can*?" said the witch, looking offended. "Really, Daniel, you go too far. And actually I was going to change Basil back in any case, sooner or later, because babies aren't really wicked. To be wicked you have to know right from wrong and choose wrong, and babies can't do that. But I cannot believe that the Boothroyds wouldn't rather have the little dog for a night or two. He's completely house-trained, did you know?"

"Honestly, Miss Tenbury-Smith, I'm sure they wouldn't. I'm really sure."

"Extraordinary," said the witch, shaking her head to and fro. "Well, in that case, let's see what we can do. Just wait while I change my clothes."

"Well, you seem to be right," said Heckie as they approached The Towers. "The dear Boothroyds do not sound happy."

All the lights were on and one could hear Mrs Boothroyd's screams halfway down the street.

"Oh, poor Sumi!"

"Now don't worry," said the witch, who had changed into her school blazer and pleated skirt. "I shall pretend to be a social worker. That always goes down well. Just follow me."

Inside the Boothroyds' sitting room, a fat policeman was writing things in a notebook and a thin policeman was talking to head-quarters on his walkie-talkie. Mrs Boothroyd was yelling and hiccupping and gulping by turns, and Mr Boothroyd was blustering and threatening to do awful things to Sumi's family. Sumi sat crouched on the sofa, her head in her hands. Between her shoes one could just see the dark, wet nose of the bewildered little dog.

"Now, my dear good people, what is all this about?" enquired Heckie briskly. "I found this poor boy wandering about in the street quite beside himself." She pointed to the letters WAW on her blazer. "I am from the Wellbridge Association for Welfare," she went on, "and we cannot be doing with that kind of thing."

"My baby's been kidnapped! My little treasure! My bobbikins!" screeched Mrs Boothroyd.

"And it's all these children's fault!" roared Mr Boothroyd.

"Nonsense," said Heckie. "He'll just have got mislaid somewhere. It often happens with babies."

"We've searched high and low, Miss," said the fat policeman.

But the little bulldog had heard Heckie's voice. He crawled out from under the sofa and as she crouched down to him, he leapt on to her lap.

"Who let that brute in again?" raged Mr Boothroyd – and Sumi blushed and turned her head away.

"Dogs give you fleas! They give you worms behind the eyeballs," screeched Mrs Boothroyd.

Heckie looked hard at the Boothroyds. She was angry, but she was also amazed. In spite of what Daniel had said, she hadn't really believed that they would prefer Basil to the little dog. Then she gathered up the puppy and went to the door which Daniel was holding open for her, and out into the garden.

For an animal witch, turning nice animals into silly people is much harder than the other way round. Heckie's eyes were sad as she shook off her left shoe so that her Toe of Transformation could suck power from the earth. Then she spoke softly to the bulldog, waiting till his tail stopped wagging and his eyes were closed. Only when he slept did she touch him with her Knuckle of Power and say her spells.

Ten minutes later, Heckie returned to the drawing-room. She had held the puppy close to her chest, but she carried Basil at arm's length like a tray. His nightdress was covered in black streaks, he was bawling – but he was quite unharmed.

"My lambkin, my prettikins, my darling!" shrieked Mrs Boothroyd, covering him with squelchy kisses.

"My son, my boy!" slobbered Mr Boothroyd.

"Where was he, Miss?" asked the fat policeman.

"At the back of the coal shed," said Heckie. "The obvious place to look for a baby, I'd have thought."

"But how did he get there?"

Heckie felt sorry for the fat policeman who so much wanted to have something to put in his notebook. "You want to look for a tall man with red hair, blue eyes, a black moustache, an orange anorak and purple socks. I saw him climbing over the garden wall. It'll be him who put Basil among the coals."

"But what would be the motive?" asked the policeman with the walkie-talkie.

"Oh, that's easy," said Heckie. "Revenge. Someone getting their own back. He'll have bought one of Mr Boothroyd's bath plugs and found it leaked. You know what it's like when all the hot water drains away and you're sitting in an empty tub all cold and blue with goose pimples . . ."

But when they had dropped Sumi off in the taxi Mr Boothroyd had been forced to pay for, Heckie turned to Daniel, looking thoughtful and serious.

"You know, Daniel, I shall have to change my plans entirely. I had no idea people would make such a fuss and be so unreasonable. I thought they'd come to me and say: "Please, Heckie, would you turn my drunken husband into a dear chimpanzee?" Or: "We feel that Uncle Phillip, who is a handbag snatcher, would do better as a Two-toed Sloth." That kind of thing. But now I see it isn't so. I shall have to work in the *strictest* secrecy. Evildoers will have to be *flushed out*!" She peered at Daniel. "Might one ask why you are snivelling? Is it because there's no one at home?"

Sumi's parents had been there to welcome her, but Daniel's house, as the taxi drew up, was silent and dark.

Daniel shook his head. "I don't mind being alone." He wiped away the tear in the corner of his eye. "It's that lovely bulldog. I miss him so *much*!"

Heckie examined his face in the light of the lamp. "You know, you have the right ideas. Yes, I think I might be able to use you. For I have to tell you, Daniel, that I have just had a vision. I see a band of Wickedness Hunters! Children and witches together, uniting to rid Wellbridge of Wickedness! Yes, yes, I see it all. But first, dear boy, I must get myself a familiar. What a good thing that tomorrow is Sunday. Come after breakfast and we'll go to the zoo!"

The Enchanted Toad

Judy Corbalis

There was once a king who had a daughter called Princess Grizelda. Princess Grizelda was rather quiet and didn't say very much but she was very very stubborn and determined once she had decided on something.

The Queen, her mother, had left their home at the palace many years before, when Grizelda was a small girl, to seek her fortune as a racing driver, so the king had had to bring up his daughter himself.

"Grizelda," he said to her one day, "I have a serious problem to discuss with you. Come into the blue drawing room."

The Princess sighed, put down her bow and arrows and followed him.

"What is it, Papa?"

"Grizelda," said the king, "it's time you were married."

"But I'm only fourteen, Papa," protested the princess.

"What do you mean – 'only fourteen'?" said the king crossly. "Fourteen's quite old enough to be married."

"But I don't *want* to be married, Papa."

"Well, sooner or later you'll have to be," said the king, "so why not now?"

"I don't know if I ever want to be married, Papa."

"What nonsense!" shouted the king. "Everyone wants to be married. Why I was married at twenty and your mother was married at fifteen."

"I know, Papa," said the princess, "and when she was eighteen she went off to race cars and we haven't seen her since."

"Well, she always sends you a birthday present," said the king defensively.

"Yes, I know, but I'd rather *see* her sometimes."

"Grizelda," said the king, "you are not to

talk about Mama. You know it only upsets me. I'm not going to listen if you do. And I want you, in fact I'm ordering you, to start thinking about who you want to marry. Because if you don't come up with some good suggestions yourself, I shall have to choose for you."

And he stormed out of the blue drawing room.

"Oh dear," said Grizelda to herself, "Now I really *do* have a problem."

She thought about all the neighbouring princes but she really couldn't face the thought of marrying any of them.

"Well," asked the king at dinner, "have you decided, Grizelda?"

"Really, Papa, you only asked me to think about it five hours ago."

The king stamped his foot and his soup plate rattled.

"Five hours is long enough for anyone," he thundered.

"Not for me, Papa," said the princess calmly. "And you've spilt your soup."

"Oh, be quiet!" shouted the king and he slammed out of the royal dining room.

The princess ate the rest of her dinner in thoughtful silence.

Next day she had breakfast in her room, got dressed in her best golden dress and slipped outdoors in her blue silk cloak.

"Your Highness," said the Court Usher as she passed him on the stairs, "have you remembered that His Majesty has asked several kings and queens from neighbouring kingdoms to lunch with him today? He particularly wanted Your Highness to be present."

The princess nodded.

"Thank you for reminding me," she said, and to herself she thought, "He's asked them because he thinks they might be interested in marrying me off to one of their sons."

And she carried on downstairs even faster.

She stayed in the gardens for an hour or two, then slipped back into the palace and up to her bedroom unnoticed. She had just enough time to sort out one or two things before lunch.

There was a blast of trumpets from downstairs.

"That'll be the heralds announcing the arrival of the other monarchs," said Princess Grizelda aloud and she smoothed her golden dress, picked up something in her hand and set off for the main staircase and the royal reception room.

"The Princess Grizelda," announced the Court Usher.

"My dear!" cried the king and he walked up and embraced her warmly. "Behave yourself, please," he muttered in her ear.

"I always do, Papa," said the princess.

"And this," announced the king, leading her forward, "is my daughter, Grizelda, my only child, who will, naturally, inherit the kingdom in due course and who, I really feel, is just of an age to be married."

The royal guests smiled at her. The princess smiled back. She took a deep breath.

"Papa," she said loudly, taking a step forward, "I've found a husband for myself."

"Really, Grizelda?" said the king. "I am surprised. And who is the lucky young man going to be?"

"It isn't a *young man*, Papa," said the

139

princess. "I met him in the garden this morning and brought him in to lunch with me."

The king was curious.

"Let him come in!" he commanded, "so we can all see this mysterious fellow. Met him in the garden, indeed! These young girls are so fanciful."

The princess went out to the hallway, picked up a small box she had deposited there and carried it in.

"Well?" demanded the king. "Where is he then?"

The princess lifted the lid of the box.

"Here, Papa."

The king looked in the box.

"It's a toad!!"

"Yes, I know, Papa, I've fallen in love with it and I'm going to marry it."

"GRIZELDA!" thundered the king.

"Lunch is served, Sire," announced the footman appearing at the door.

One of the visiting kings leaned over to Grizelda's father and whispered in his ear, "I shouldn't discourage her too hard if I were you. It will almost certainly be a prince under enchantment."

The king was doubtful.

"Are you sure?"

"They always are," said the visiting king. "Let her have him on the table at lunch and have your Court Wizard change him back later on."

"What a splendid idea," said the king. "Thank you. I hadn't thought of that."

"There have been dozens of cases exactly like it," pointed out the visiting king.

So the Princess Grizelda took her toad in to lunch and it sat by her golden plate as she fed it with tiny scraps of her own food.

The visitors left in the early afternoon. Grizelda shook hands with them all and smiled prettily. The toad looked at them with its unblinking eyes.

The king felt a light touch on his shoulder.

"Don't forget. Get the enchanter in right away," murmured his friend.

The king nodded.

"And many thanks," he said gratefully.

"Don't mention it," said the visiting king.

The princess took her toad into the library.

She was examining its warts when the herald arrived with a message that she and the toad were wanted in the throne room.

"The throne room!" The princess was impressed. "Something special must be happening."

"His Majesty is in full regalia," announced the herald importantly.

"Really? It must be something vital then. I wonder what it can be?" said the princess, and picking up her toad she set off along the palace corridor.

The throne room door was opened by the Chief Usher. Inside the room were the King, the Lord Chamberlain, the Court Jester, the Chief Judge and the Court Enchanter. The Court Enchanter was considered to be one of the best wizards in the world. He was always going off to perform difficult spells or to change people back into their normal shapes or to magick someone or something somewhere.

People said he could conjure up all sorts of wonderful things and nobody wanted to get on the wrong side of him because it was reputed that he had once put a bad spell on someone who had offended him and caused lizards to jump out of her mouth every time she opened it.

Grizelda went into the room.

"Good afternoon, Papa," she greeted him, and she smiled and nodded at his retinue.

"Good afternoon, my dear," said the king and, looking at the toad, he said, obviously making a great effort, "and how is my future son-in-law this afternoon?"

"Oh, very well, thank you, Papa."

"Good," said the king.

"Would you like to stroke him, Papa?"

"No, no thanks!" said the king hastily. "Ah, I'm sure he's ah, very, ah, friendly, yes, I'm sure he's got a wonderful nature and so on, but, ah, I don't think I'll stroke him just yet, thank you, Grizelda.

"Now," he went on, "the reason I've brought you down here is because I happen to believe your toad, that is, my son-in-law to be, is really a prince under enchantment."

The Princess Grizelda was very disappointed.

"Oh no, Papa, I hope not!"

"Now look here, " said the king. "Don't be ridiculous, Grizelda. I mean you can get toads anywhere but princes are another thing altogether. I'll get you another toad as a wedding present if you want. And that's a promise. Now bring that toad over here and put him on the small table."

Grizelda put her toad down in front of the enchanter.

The enchanter looked at her with his piercing green eyes.

"Stand back, Your Highness," he ordered. Then, taking a huge red silk handkerchief from one pocket of his robe, and a wand from the other, he dropped the handkerchief over the toad, threw a powder from another pocket into a glass of water, poured the water over the handkerchief, then waved his wand over it, muttering strangely to himself all the time.

There was a sudden flash of pink smoke and a dull boom, the handkerchief and the toad disappeared, and in its place stood a white rabbit.

The princess was overjoyed.

"A rabbit! Oh, papa, how wonderful! I've always wanted a rabbit."

"Not for a *husband*!" bellowed the king, enraged.

And to the enchanter he said nastily, "You'll have to do something considerably better than that!"

The enchanter turned his piercing green eyes towards the king.

"Patience, Your Highness. These things are very skilled and take time."

"I can see that," said the king bitterly.

The enchanter pulled out another hand-kerchief, a blue one this time, and laid it over the rabbit.

"Oh no, please don't, please don't." The princess was distressed.

The enchanter put his hand deep in his robe, pulled out a tiny top hat, and presented it to her.

"Here you are," he said gravely. "Put your hand in there."

Grizelda could only get two fingers into the hat because it was so small. Feeling something soft and furry, she pulled at it.

Out popped the tiniest baby rabbit she had ever seen.

"For you," said the enchanter. "A present to make up for losing this one."

"Oh thank you!" cried Princess Grizelda and she put the baby rabbit back in the hat for safe keeping and put the hat in her pocket.

The enchanter was busy with his spell. He had taken out a large book from behind the throne, a book Grizelda was sure had never been there before, and was studying it intently.

146

Suddenly he leaned forward towards the king.

"Excuse me, Your Majesty," he said, reached behind the king's ear and pulled out a large lemon.

"Oh dear," he said, and reaching behind the king's other ear, pulled out an enormous black spider.

"Stop it *at once!*" commanded the king. "And that's an order."

"Sorry, Your Majesty," murmured the enchanter. "I just thought you'd like to know they were there."

"Thank you for that consideration," said the king. "Now get on with the job."

The enchanter plucked a star from out of the air above his head, laid it on the blue handkerchief, twirled three times round on his toes, and shouted "Abracadabra!"

There was a blinding flash of green light and, lo and behold, a beautiful red sportscar appeared before them.

"My gosh!" breathed Grizelda.

The Lord Chancellor leaned forward enviously. "I'd like that," he sighed.

The king looked very hard at the enchanter. "I see: a sportscar."

"Well, yes," said the enchanter, "I told Your Majesty these things take time."

"Look," said the king through clenched teeth, "I cannot have a sportscar as a son-in-law. The princess cannot marry a *sportscar*."

His voice rose to a shriek. "WHOEVER HEARD OF A KINGDOM RULED BY A SPORTS-CAR?"

"A passing bagatelle, Your Majesty," said the enchanter hastily. "We're almost there now."

"It's a very beautiful sportscar," pointed out the princess.

"Grizelda . . .," said the king warningly.

The Lord Chamberlain broke in. "Your Majesty, the enchanter is about to try again."

"He'd better," said the king.

The enchanter took out a checked tablecloth from the back pocket of his robe and flung it over the sportscar.

The Lord Chamberlain sighed. "What a pity."

The king shot him a furious look.

The enchanter lifted three lizards out of a banqueting dish on the regalia table and laid them on the cloth. He took a vial of red liquid from his sleeve, shook it over the lizards and waved his wand low over them.

A tongue of flame shot into the air. Everybody screamed and jumped back.

The smoke cleared and there before them lay – a fish finger.

"NO, NO, NO, NO," groaned the king. "THERE IS NO SUCH THING AS A KINGDOM RULED BY A FISH FINGER! I'm *not* having a fish finger as a son-in-law. I'd rather have a toad. Take him away!" he shouted, pointing at the enchanter. "Off with his head and bring it to me on a plate! It'll be a pleasure, I can tell you."

"Papa!" The princess was deeply shocked. "What a *terrible* thing to say."

The enchanter burst into tears. He reached into his other sleeve and brought out a placard saying,

Wife and Six Children to Support.

"You won't get my sympathy *that* way," said the king. "My mind is made up. Take him away!"

The Princess Grizelda jumped to her feet and stood in front of her father.

"I won't have it, Papa," she cried sternly. "This was all your idea in the first place and it wasn't even your toad. It was mine. Of course you're not going to chop off his head. You're going to give him one last chance to succeed and if he doesn't, you're going to send him on a month's holiday."

"That's just encouraging him to fail," said the king.

"Honestly, Sire," said the enchanter, "it was just a temporary setback. I've prepared my next and final spell now. I *am* in the entertainment business, Sire, after all."

"Entertainment!" exploded the king. "You call this entertainment?"

"Stop it, at once, both of you," ordered the princess. And turning to the enchanter she said, "Would you please try again now?"

"And you'd better get it right this time," snorted the king.

"I will," the enchanter assured them.

He pulled a purple silken cloth with golden

stars on it from the Chief Judge's trouser leg and laid it over the fish finger. Then he reached inside his own mouth, pulled out a tonsil and laid that on the cloth.

"Yuk!" said the king. "How disgusting!"

"But effective, Sire," replied the enchanter. "And now, please, absolute silence."

He bent down on his knees, crossed his fingers, his toes and his eyes and breathed on the tonsil.

The tonsil quivered and grew and grew. The purple cloth with golden stars rose and flapped and shook until it seemed to fill the room. There was a boom of thunder and a light like the sun dazzled them all.

"How beautiful!" murmured the princess to herself.

Suddenly there was a jolt and a bang and without warning they all flew up to the ceiling and fell to the ground again. The room grew dark.

"Sorry about this," came the enchanter's voice through the gloom. "We're nearly there."

A misty cloud was gathering in the middle

of the room. A dim human shape was forming inside it.

The enchanter sighed inaudibly with relief, the king muttered aloud, "At last!"

And the Princess Grizelda said to herself, "I do hope he's nice and he likes having fun."

The cloud began to dispel, the light slowly returned to normal and the figure emerged more clearly until it stood visible to them all.

"GOOD HEAVENS!" bellowed the king. "It's Marguerite!"

"Hello, darling," said the figure.

"Mother!" shouted Grizelda and threw herself into the stranger's arms.

"And where have *you* been for the last eleven years then, if it's not a rude question?" asked the king.

"Oh, Arthur," said the queen, holding Grizelda tightly, "don't go on and on, please. I thought you'd be so pleased to see me again. I've been away seeking my fortune, of course, I'm an extremely famous racing driver."

"Well, I've never heard of you," announced the king, "and I've checked the racing lists every time there's been a Grand Prix."

"Oh, Arthur. Did you!" The queen was touched. "That is romantic of you."

The king blushed.

"But," went on the queen, "I raced under an assumed name of course, otherwise people might have thought my winning was favouritism. And, Grizelda," she continued, "it's so wonderful to see you at last, my darling. I've wanted and wanted to come back, but I knew I couldn't until I'd proved myself. And I've finally done it."

The Princess Grizelda clung tighter to her mother's neck.

"Oh, Mama, I'm so glad you're back at last."

"What I don't understand," said the king, "is if you've reached the peak of your career, what on earth you were doing in the palace garden disguised as a toad. And then to put me through that dreadful business of the rabbit and the sportscar and the fish finger! It's a wonder I'm not grey with worry and strain."

"Well, I couldn't help it," explained the queen. She turned to the enchanter. "It was a terribly strong spell. You did marvellously well to break it at all."

The enchanter looked modest.

"It was nothing, Your Highness."

"It was everything to *me*," the queen assured him. "I could have just about coped with spending the rest of my life as a pet rabbit or a sportscar and at least I would have been at the palace. But a fish finger! I ask you? Here one day and gobbled up the next. I was quite terrified. I was shaking in my breadcrumbs."

"Oh, Mama," breathed Grizelda, "just imagine if the enchanter had failed and we'd eaten you up for tea."

Her eyes filled with tears at the thought.

"Well, we didn't," said the king cheerfully, "so stop crying, Grizelda."

He came and put his arm round the queen and kissed her cheek.

"I'm so glad you've come back."

"I shall never go off again now, I can tell you," promised the queen, "though I had some fun while I was racing."

"Will you tell me all about it?" asked Grizelda eagerly.

"Later," promised the queen.

"We must have a banquet and a party to celebrate your return," said the king, "but there's still one thing I don't understand. How did you come to be a toad?"

"Well," explained the queen, "I was racing very well indeed and clearly I was going to win the major prize. The only person who was anywhere near as good as I was, was a driver who had been a wizard and had given it up for racing, but he was still not up to my standard. And when I had won the competition and it came to the presentation of the prizes, he was so jealous that he cast a spell over me and changed me into a toad, and it took me seven months to hop hack here to the palace and then it wasn't till this morning, when Grizelda found me, that anyone noticed me at all, and, of course, you know the rest of the story."

"Amazing," said the king.

"That wizard should be punished," said the Chief Judge.

"He will be," promised the king. "I shall make a point of it."

"Well, if everyone is happy now," put in the

enchanter, "I'd quite like to be getting off home to my own family . . ."

"Just a moment," said the king sternly. "You promised me a husband for the princess and I haven't got one. She can't marry her mother."

"With respect, Sire," said the enchanter, "*you* asked me if I could change a toad into a prince and I said I'd do my best. I rather thought," he went on huffily, "that I'd done better than my best, but of course if Your Majesty disagrees . . ."

"Absolutely. You've done *marvellously*," cried the queen, "and I shall personally see about a reward in due course."

The enchanter smiled gratefully.

"I still don't know how I'm going to get Grizelda a husband though," muttered the king.

"A husband!" The queen was incredulous. "What on earth does she want a *husband* for? She's only fourteen."

"I don't," put in Grizelda hastily.

"I should think *not*," said the queen. "I've never heard such nonsense. I married young, and look what happened to me. You're surely not encouraging her, Arthur?"

"Well, what else is she going to do?" asked the king defensively.

"What do you want to do, Grizelda?" asked her mother.

Grizelda thought for a bit.

"Well, Mama," she said finally, "what I'd like to do first is to stay here with you for a while and play with my rabbit, and the toad Papa has promised me, and then there is something I'd really like to do."

"And what is that?"

"I hope you won't think it's silly," said the princess, "but I'd simply *love* to be an astronaut. I've always wanted to be one."

"I've never heard of anything so ridiculous," said the king.

"I think it's a wonderfully exciting idea," said the queen, "and you should certainly be allowed to try it. And now, Arthur," she continued, turning to the king, "if it's possible, and I'm sure it should be, I'd love something to eat. I'm so sick of slugs and snails and worms."

157

"Oh, my dear," cried the king remorsefully, "of course, of course. I'm so sorry. I completely forgot about it in the shock of the moment. Yes. At once. Let's all three of us have a special celebration meal together tonight. I'm so delighted to have you back again."

"And so am I, Mama," murmured the Princess Grizelda, snuggling up to her mother.

"It seems to me," said the enchanter to himself, "that this time I've made an entirely satisfactory job of things."

And wrapping his cloak tightly round himself, he waved a hasty goodbye to everyone and slipped out of the palace off home to his own supper.

How Not to be a Giant Killer

David Henry Wilson

Jack's big mistake was to try to make a comeback. Having retired as undefeated giant-killing champion of Cornwall, he should have left it at that. After all, he'd married the Duke's daughter, and one day he would be Duke himself. No worries about money, housing, unemployment – Jack had it made. But once a fighter, always a fighter. He started longing for the bright lights, the publicity, and razzamatazz of the giant-killing game, and at last he could stand it no longer and informed his wife that he was going out to kill a giant.

"Ts!" tutted Charlotte. "Just when I've

put the dinner on!"

"I can't help that," said Jack. "A man's gotta do what a man's gotta do."

"Anyway," said Charlotte, "I thought you'd killed off all the giants already."

"In Cornwall I have," said Jack. "But there must be plenty left in Devon."

"Who wants to go to Devon?" snorted Charlotte.

"I do," said Jack. "To kill a giant."

And off he went to look for his horse, his sword and his cloak. You may remember that a grateful wizard had given Jack a horse that could run like the wind, a sword that could cut through anything, and a cloak that made its wearer invisible. The horse was out in the field grazing, as it had been doing for the last three years. When Jack climbed on its back and said "Giddy up!" the horse took one heavy step forward and its tummy bumped the ground.

"Can you still run like the wind?" asked Jack.

"I can't run at all," replied the horse. "Though I do have plenty of wind."

"Ah, well," said Jack, "I'll just have to walk. The exercise'll do me good."

Next, he searched for his sword, which he found in the garden shed under the lawn-mower. It had gone rusty. When Jack tried to cut the head off a dandelion with it, the blade snapped and fell off the handle.

"Ah, well," said Jack, "I'll just have to use my brains and my invisible cloak."

But he couldn't see his invisible cloak anywhere.

"It must have disappeared," said Jack. "Ah,

well, I'll just have to move so fast that they can't see me. I'm off now, dear."

"Well, try and get back for dinner," said Charlotte.

Devon had only been three or four inches away on the map, but by dinner-time Jack was still in Cornwall and was feeling tired and hungry. He knocked on a nearby door, and a man opened it.

"Hullo," said Jack. "I'm Jack the Giant-Killer."

"And I'm the Duke of Cornwall," said the man, and shut the door in Jack's face.

The man in the next house said he was the King's grandfather, and the people in the third house had a little dog with giant-killing ideas of its own. Jack was lucky to escape with nothing worse than a torn trouser-seat. He gave up knocking on doors, and walked sadly on with aching feet, a rumbling tum, and a cold bottom. He walked all through the night until at last he came to a sign which said, *Welcome to Devon*.

"Some welcome!" said Jack, and flopped down exhausted at the side of the road and went to sleep.

As he slept, Jack dreamt that he was still knocking on people's doors, and he kept calling out: "I'm Jack the Giant-Killer! I'm the Duke's son-in-law!" But nobody believed him in his dream either.

The next morning, two Devon giants named Klottid and Kreem happened to come along the road. Just as they drew close to Jack, he cried out, "I'm Jack the Giant-Killer! I'm the Duke's son-in-law!"

"I've heard of him," said Klottid. "He killed all the giants in Cornwall."

"In that case," said Kreem, "we'd better stop him from killing all the giants in Devon."

When Jack finally woke up, he knew that he must be very ill, because he couldn't move a muscle.

"Help! Help!" he cried. "I'm paralysed! Call the doctor!"

There were two gigantic laughs and Jack, who was bound hand and foot (and every-where else), was just able to turn his head enough to see the smiling faces of Klottid and Kreem.

"Jack the Giant-Killer, are you?" said Klottid.

"That's right," said Jack. "And I'm very ill ... I'm ..."

"Oh, dearie, dearie me," said Kreem. "Now which of us are you going to kill first?"

Jack suddenly realized that he was the prisoner of two giants.

"Oh!" he said. "Ah! Um! Well ... no ... look ... I've retired! That's it ... I've retired from killing giants."

"Ooh, thank Heavens for that!" said Klottid.

"What a relief!" said Kreem.

"So you've got nothing to be afraid of," said Jack.

"Ooh, what a relief!" said Klottid.

"Thank Heavens for that!" said Kreem.

"Mind you, Kreemy," said Klottid, "I knew he was *bound* to leave us alone!"

"Oh, so did I, Klotty," said Kreem. "He's much too tied up to bother about us!"

"So you can let me go," said Jack, "and I'll be on my way."

"What a sense of humour!" said Klottid.

"All those Cornish giants must have died

laughing!" said Kreem.

Then they put poor tied-up Jack in a box (thus making him the very first Jack-in-the-box) and invited all their friends to come and see. In those days there weren't very many giants-killers in captivity, and so before long giants were coming from all over the country (except Cornwall) to look and laugh. Klottid and Kreem charged them an entrance fee, and also served delicious teas in their front parlour. (Klottid Kreem Teas are still a tradition in Devon today.) There were soon Jack-the Giant-Killer mugs and plates and T-shirts, *A History of Jack's Capture* – written by the famous historian, Liza Plenty – and a do-it-yourself Giant-Killer-Capture-Kit, which consisted of a signed picture of Klottid and Kreem, plus a piece of string. Business boomed, and everyone was happy. Everyone, that is, except Jack.

Day after day, week after week, Jack lay in his box thinking up escape plans. His first idea was to threaten the giants.

"If you don't let me go," he warned them, "you'll be in a lot of trouble."

"What sort of trouble?" asked the giants.

That was a question Jack couldn't answer, and so he abandoned the idea. His next plan was to challenge them to a fight – him against them, with no holds barred. They sportingly accepted the challenge and untied him. Then they tied him up again, and that was the end of that.

With plan number three he pretended to be dead. He reckoned they would untie him and throw him away, so he lay very still in his box.

"Definitely dead," said Klottid.

"Dead as a Cornish giant," said Kreem.

Jack's heart fluttered with hope.

"He's starting to smell already," said Klottid.

"We'll throw him on the fire straight away," said Kreem.

Jack miraculously came back to life, and that was the end of plan three.

Obviously these Devon giants were a lot less stupid than Cornish giants. They were making a fortune. They'd scared any other giant-killers out of Devon, and they seemed to have made escape impossible. What was needed was a super plan. And a super plan is what Jack eventually found.

Like all the best ideas, it was simple, though unlike all the best ideas, it did have one tiny flaw. The plan was to do nothing. One day, as Jack correctly reasoned, the giants would die and then someone might come and release him. Not only was this his best chance, but it was also his only chance, and so Jack settled down for a long wait.

The one tiny flaw in Jack's plan showed itself just twenty years later. Instead of the giants dying, it was Jack who died. This was quite unexpected, and he would have been rather upset about it if he had still been alive. Nobody knew exactly what he had died of, so the doctor wrote that the cause of death was Loss of Life, which seemed to cover everything. The giants duly untied him and threw him away – as he had foreseen in plan three – but being untied and being free was not much use to him now that he was dead.

When news of his death eventually reached Charlotte, she took his dinner out of the oven and ate it herself.

"Twenty-one years I've been keeping it warm for him," she told her father, "and I'm certainly not going to waste it now."

As for the giants, they lived on for another twenty years, and finally died of old age, both on the same day. Their friends erected a tombstone for them, on which was written:

Here lie the giants, Klottid and Kreem,
Who earned their place in Heaven
By making sure that giant-killers
Never killed in Devon.

And since that time, no giant has ever been killed by a giant-killer in Devon.

Mrs Anancy, Chicken Soup and Anancy

James Berry

Mrs Anancy has six chickens she fat-
tened up to sell. She wants the money
to get a dress to wear to a special church
service. Anancy makes himself believe Mrs
Anancy has enough nice dresses already.

Anancy whispers to himself, "Oh, those fat
and lovely chickens! They'll be much, much
nicer in one special meal. Any good and
loving husband deserves that. Any one! But,
oh, there is the trouble. Mrs Anancy will
never, never agree."

Bro Nancy works out a way for the six fat
chickens to become his meal.

Anancy goes and sees Bro Dog. Anancy

gets Bro Dog to agree to go and do a little trick job for him.

Bro Dog goes and hides himself in the doctor's surgery. He stays there hidden till the surgery is closed.

Just before night comes down, Mrs Anancy walks into her home. She comes and finds her husband close to death, in pain.

"Oh, my husband, what's the matter? What's the matter?"

"Oh, my wife – good-good wife – pain has me in its jaws. Pain chews me up. Pain cuts me up. Everywhere." Anancy clutches himself and rolls about in the bed.

"My poor-poor husband. Where is the pain? Where?"

"Everywhere," Anancy groans. "In my belly, in my throat, in my mouth, on my tongue, there's a blazing fire."

"I must get the doctor," Mrs Anancy says, all worried.

Anancy groans. Anancy sobs. Anancy gasps, "Wife – I'm getting a glimpse – a glimpse – of another world. A light – a light beckons me to another place."

"No, no, husband. Don't go." Mrs Anancy embraces her husband. "Hold on. Hold on. I'm going to the doctor. Right away. Right away."

Anancy keeps up his tired groans. Then, as Mrs Anancy is ready to rush out of the house, he says, "Good wife, you must hurry. But – but – but I'm getting terrible signs. Please. Please don't take any short cuts. No short cuts, good wife. None. There are pits hidden. There are trees with roots loosened. There are rocks on hillsides, propped by few rotten leaves."

"Every word is taken, good husband. Every

word is taken. Now I must go." Mrs Anancy leaves the house in haste.

Then sudden-sudden Mrs Anancy stops. She doesn't want to leave Bro Nancy alone. She looks back at the house. A little way further along she looks back at the yard. In disbelief, she sees Bro Nancy rush out onto the road. He goes the other way, hurrying. He turns in on to the short cut.

Mrs Anancy is puzzled. She turns round and follows Anancy.

At first Mrs Anancy is worried. Her husband may be driven by his illness to do something crazy. Then she realises he's surely heading for the doctor's surgery. Wondering what Bro Nancy is going to do Mrs Anancy follows unseen. And to keep up with his speed she has to put in bursts of running.

At the surgery the place is closed. Then Bro Dog comes out and receives Bro Nancy. Both go back inside and lights are put on. Mrs Anancy stands outside in shocking disbelief. Nothing is wrong with her husband. He and Bro Dog talk happily inside.

Not knowing exactly what to do, Mrs

Anancy stands outside waiting and thinking for a while.

Then Mrs Anancy goes to the surgery door and knocks. Doctor comes and asks her in.

Doctor is a bearded and bent-back little old man. Doctor wears dark glasses and a white coat. Doctor speaks in a peculiar croaking voice.

"It's my husband, Doctor," Mrs Anancy says. "He's at home in bed in terrible, terrible pain."

"Does he have pains everywhere?" Doctor asks in his peculiar croaking voice.

"Yes, Doctor."

"The pains come worst in the belly and throat and mouth and tongue?"

"Yes, Doctor."

"Common. Very common." Doctor shakes head. "Some bad-bad cases about."

"Will he be cured, Doctor?"

"Yes, yes. Completely. But there's only one cure."

"Yes, Doctor? Tell me."

"Chicken soup. Go home, Mrs Anancy. Find six to eight of the fattest chickens. Make the tastiest soup you ever made. Give every bit of it to the patient, every bit of flesh and soup and seasoning. And leave him alone to eat, madam. Leave him alone."

"Thank you, sir."

Mrs Anancy conceals herself outside. She sees the surgery lights go out. She sees Bro Nancy and Bro Dog slip away smart-smart.

Mrs Anancy gets home. There is singing inside. She stands. She listens to every bit of Anancy's song:

> "*A big-big good lot*
> *Can make you fat-fat.*
> *Why be one of you*
> *And not two of you?*
> *Why be one of you, O?*
> *And not two of you, O? . . ."*

Wanting Anancy to hear her, Mrs Anancy goes inside nosily. Instant-instant, the singing stops. She goes into the room. Anancy rolls about, groaning in pain.

"Any news? Any good news, good wife?"

"I'm to give you chicken soup."

"That'll cure me?"

"I'm to give you lots of it. Lots of it."

"Oh! Oh!" Anancy groans. "When will the treatment start?"

"Not tonight."

Early morning Mrs Anancy goes and sees Dora. She comes back, kills the six chickens and begins the cooking.

Mrs Anancy makes herself very busy. Importantly, she goes and opens Anancy's bedroom window. Mrs Anancy sets up her cooking just outside, under the window. The cooking steams up more and more. Tempting cooking smells drift in and fill Anancy's room.

With the delicious cooking under his nose, Bro Nancy turns and twists. He turns his face to the wall. He turns his face the other way. He turns his face towards the ceiling. Sometimes Bro Nancy sits up in bed. When he hears Mrs Anancy round at the back, he craftily takes a peep outside at the cooking.

Anancy lies down. Part of his song comes into his head:

"A big-big good lot
Can make you fat-fat . . ."

Mrs Anancy sets up a long table outside, near her cooking. She goes and closes Anancy's window. She tells him, "I don't want to tempt you any more. I don't want you to either see or smell the spiced-up soup. Everything is ready. Just wait."

Anancy continues his long wait.

Unseen by Anancy, Dora arrives with a party of village children. Dora settles the twenty-four children around the long table. Picked out as the worst fed, they wait with ravenous appetites.

Mrs Anancy dishes up every bit of the chicken flesh and soup and seasoning. All is put in front of the children. In no time every bit is eaten up. Every bowl is left clean.

Tortured by sounds outside, and his waiting-waiting, Anancy leaps up, swings the window open and rushes outside.

Anancy sees the children and their empty bowls. He sees the big empty iron pot. He sees everybody looking at him. Anancy holds his head and screams, "My chicken soup! My chicken soup!"

The children burst out singing:

> "*A big-big good lot*
> *Can make you fat-fat.*
> *Why be one of you*
> *And not two of you?*
> *Why be one of you*
> *And not two of you?*
> *Anancy, O!*
> *Anancy, O! . . ."*

Anancy storms out of the yard. But he doesn't stay away for long. He is simply too hungry.

Send Three and Fourpence We are Going to a Dance

Jan Mark

Mike and Ruth Dixon got on well enough, but not so well that they wanted to walk home from school together. Ruth would not have minded, but Mike, who was two classes up, preferred to amble along with his friends so that he usually arrived a long while after Ruth did.

Ruth was leaning out of the kitchen window when he came in through the side gate, kicking a brick.

"I've got a message for you," said Mike. "From school. Miss Middleton wants you to

178

go and see her tomorrow before assembly, and take a dead frog."

"What's she want *me* to take a dead frog for?" said Ruth. "She's not my teacher. I haven't got a dead frog."

"How should I know?" Mike let himself in. "Where's Mum?"

"Round Mrs Todd's. Did she really say a dead frog? I mean, really say it?"

"Derek told me to tell you. It's nothing to do with me."

Ruth cried easily. She cried now. "I bet she never. You're pulling my leg."

"I'm not, and you'd better do it. She said it was important – Derek said – and you know what a rotten old temper she's got," said Mike, feelingly.

"But why me? It's not fair." Ruth leaned her head on the window sill and wept in earnest. "Where'm I going to find a dead frog?"

"Well, you can peel them off the road sometimes when they've been run over. They go all dry and flat like pressed flowers," said Mike. He did think it a trifle unreasonable to demand dead frogs from little girls, but Miss

Middleton *was* unreasonable. Everyone knew that. "You could start a pressed frog collection," he said.

Ruth sniffed fruitily. "What do you think Miss'll do if I don't get one?"

"She'll go barmy, that's what," said Mike. "She's barmy anyway," he said. "Nah, don't start howling again. Look, I'll go down the ponds after tea. I know there's frogs there because I saw the spawn, back at Easter."

"But those frogs are alive. She wants a dead one."

"I dunno. Perhaps we could get it put to sleep or something, like Mrs Todd's Tibby was. And don't tell Mum. She doesn't like me down the ponds and she won't let us have frogs indoors. Get an old box with a lid and leave it on the rockery, and I'll put old Froggo in it when I come home. *And stop crying!*"

After Mike had gone out Ruth found the box that her summer sandals had come in. She poked air holes in the top and furnished it with damp grass and a tin lid full of water. Then she left it on the rockery with a length of darning wool so that Froggo could be fastened down safely until morning. It was only possible to imagine Froggo alive; all tender and green and saying croak-croak. She could not think of him dead and flat and handed over to Miss Middleton, who definitely must have gone barmy. Perhaps Mike or Derek had been wrong about the dead part. She hoped they had.

She was in the bathroom, getting ready for bed, when Mike came home. He looked round the door and stuck up his thumbs.

"Operation Frog successful. Over and out."

"Wait. Is he . . . alive?"

"Shhh. Mum's in the hall. Yes."

"What's he like?"

"Sort of frog-shaped. Look, I've got him; OK? I'm going down now."

"Is he green."

"No. More like that pork pie that went mouldy on top. Good night!"

Mike had hidden Froggo's dungeon under the front hedge, so all Ruth had to do next morning was scoop it up as she went out of the gate. Mike had left earlier with his friends, so she paused for a moment to introduce herself. She tapped quietly on the lid. "Hullo?"

There was no answering cry of croak-croak. Perhaps he *was* dead. Ruth felt a tear coming and raised the lid a fraction at one end. There was a scrabbling noise and at the other end of the box she saw something small and alive, crouching in the grass.

"Poor Froggo," she whispered through the air holes. "I won't let her kill you, I promise," and she continued on her way to school feeling brave and desperate, and ready to protect Froggo's life at the cost of her own.

The school was in the middle of the building and classrooms opened off it. Miss Middleton had Class Three this year, next to the cloakroom. Ruth hung up her blazer, untied the wool from Froggo's box and went to meet her doom. Miss Middleton was arranging little stones in an aquarium on top of the bookcase, and jerked her head when Ruth knocked, to show that she should come in.

"I got him, Miss," said Ruth, holding out the shoebox in trembling hands.

"What, dear?" said Miss Middleton, up to her wrists in water-weed.

"Only he's not dead and I won't let you kill him!" Ruth cried, and swept off the lid with a dramatic flourish. Froggo, who must have been waiting for this, sprung out, towards Miss Middleton, landed with a clammy sound on that vulnerable place between the collar bones, and slithered down inside Miss Middleton's blouse.

Miss Middleton taught Nature Study. She was not afraid of little damp creatures, but she was not expecting Froggo. She gave a squawk of alarm and jumped backwards. The aquarium skidded in the opposite direction; took off; shattered against a desk. The contents broke over Ruth's new sandals in a tidal wave, and Lily the goldfish thrashed about in a shallow puddle on the floor. People came running with mops and dustpans. Lily Fish was taken out by the tail to recover in the cloakroom sink. Froggo was arrested while trying to leave Miss Middleton's blouse through the gap between two buttons, and put back in his box with a

weight on top in case he made another dash for freedom.

Ruth, crying harder than she had ever done in her life, was sent to stand outside the Headmaster's room, accused of playing stupid practical jokes; and cruelty to frogs.

*

Sir looked rather as if he had been laughing, but it seemed unlikely, under the circumstances, and Ruth's eyes were so swollen and tear-filled that she couldn't see clearly. He gave her a few minutes to dry out and then said, "This isn't like you, Ruth. Whatever possessed you to go throwing frogs at poor Miss Middleton? And poor frog, come to that."

"She told me to bring her a frog," said Ruth, stanching another tear at the injustice of it all. "Only she wanted a dead one, and I couldn't find a dead one, and I couldn't kill Froggo. I won't kill him," she said, remembering her vow on the way to school.

"Miss Middleton says she did not ask you to bring her a frog, or kill her a frog. She thinks you've been very foolish and unkind," said Sir, "and I think you are not telling the truth. Now . . ."

"Mike told me to," said Ruth.

"Your brother? Oh, come now."

"He did. He said Miss Middleton wanted me to go to her before assembly with a dead frog and I did, only it wasn't dead and I won't!"

185

"Ruth! Don't grizzle. No one is going to murder your frog, but we must get this nonsense sorted out." Sir opened his door and called to a passer-by, "Tell Michael Dixon that I want to see him at once, in my office."

Mike arrived, looking wary. He had heard the crash and kept out of the way, but a summons from Sir was not to be ignored.

"Come in, Michael," said Sir. "Now, why did you tell your sister that Miss Middleton wanted her to bring a dead frog to school?"

"It wasn't me," said Mike. "It was a message from Miss Middleton."

"Miss Middleton told you?"

"No, Derek Bingham told me. She told him to tell me – I suppose," said Mike, sulkily. He scowled at Ruth. All her fault.

"Then you'd better fetch Derek Bingham here right away. We're going to get to the bottom of this."

Derek arrived. He too had heard the crash.

"Come in, Derek," said Sir. "I understand that you told Michael here some tarradiddle about his sister. You let him think it was a message from Miss Middleton, didn't you?"

"Yes, well . . ." Derek shuffled. "Miss Middleton didn't tell *me*. She told, er, someone, and they told me."

"Who was this someone?"

Derek turned all noble and stood up straight and pale. "I can't remember, Sir."

"Don't let's have any heroics about sneaking, Derek, or I shall get very *cross*."

Derek's nobility ebbed rapidly. "It was Tim Hancock, Sir. He said Miss Middleton wanted Ruth Dixon to bring her a dead dog before assembly."

"A dead *dog*?"

"Yes Sir."

"Didn't you think it a bit strange that Miss Middleton should ask Ruth for a dead dog, Derek?"

"I thought she must have one, Sir."

"But why should Miss Middleton want it?"

"Well, she does do Nature Study," said Derek.

"Go and fetch Tim," said Sir.

Tim had been playing football on the field when the aquarium went down. He came in with an innocent smile which wilted when he saw what was waiting for him.

"Sir?"

"Would you mind repeating the message that you gave Derek yesterday afternoon?"

"I told him Miss Middleton wanted Sue Nixon to bring her a red sock before assembly," said Tim. "It was important."

"Red sock? Sue Nixon?" said Sir. He was beginning to look slightly wild-eyed. "Who's Sue Nixon? There's no one in this school called Sue Nixon."

"I don't know of any of the girls, Sir," said Tim.

"Didn't you think a red sock was an odd thing to ask for?"

"I thought she was bats, Sir."

"Sue Nixon?"

"No Sir. Miss Middleton, Sir," said truthful Tim.

Sir raised his eyebrows. "But why did you tell Derek?"

"I couldn't find anyone else, Sir. It was late."

"But why Derek?"

"I had to tell someone or I'd have got into trouble," said Tim, virtuously.

"You are in trouble," said Sir. "Michael, ask Miss Middleton to step in here for a moment, please."

Miss Middleton, frog-ridden, looked round the door.

"I'm sorry to bother you again," said Sir, "but it seems that Tim thinks you told him that one Sue Nixon was to bring you a red sock before assembly."

"Tim!" said Miss Middleton, very shocked. "That's a naughty fib. I never told you any such thing."

"Oh Sir," said Tim. "Miss didn't tell me. It was Pauline Bates done that."

"*Did* that. I think I see Pauline out in the hall," said Sir. "In the PT class. Yes? Let's have her in."

Pauline was very small and very frightened. Sir sat her on his knee and told her not to worry. "All we want to know," he said, "is what you said to Tim yesterday. About Sue Nixon and the dead dog."

"Red sock, Sir," said Tim.

"Sorry. Red sock. Well, Pauline?"

Pauline looked as if she might join Ruth in tears. Ruth had just realized that she was no longer involved, and was crying with relief.

"You said Miss Middleton gave you a message for Sue Nixon. What was it?"

"It wasn't Sue Nixon," said Pauline, damply. "It was June Nichols. It wasn't Miss Middleton, it was Miss Wimbledon."

"There *is* no Miss Wimbledon," said Sir. "June Nichols, yes. I know June, but Miss Wimbledon . . .?"

"She means Miss Wimpole, Sir," said Tim. "The big girls call her Wimbledon 'cause she plays tennis, Sir, in a little skirt."

"I thought you didn't know any girls," said Sir. "What did Miss Wimpole say to you, Pauline?"

"She didn't," said Pauline. "It was Moira Thatcher. She said to tell June Nichols to come and see Miss Whatsit before assembly and bring her bed socks."

"Then why tell Tim?"

"I couldn't find June. June's in his class."

"I begin to see daylight," said Sir. "Not

much, but it's there. All right, Pauline. Go and get Moira, please."

Moira had recently had a new brace fitted across her front teeth. It caught the light when she opened her mouth.

"Yeth, Thir?"

"Moira, take it slowly, and tell us what the message was about June Nichols."

Moira took a deep breath and polished the brace with her tongue.

"Well, Thir, Mith Wimpole thaid to thell June to thee her before athembly with her wed fw – thw – thth—"

"Frock?" said Sir. Moira nodded gratefully. "So why tell Pauline?"

"Pauline liveth up her thtweet, Thir."

"No I don't," said Pauline. "They moved. They got a council house, up the Ridgeway."

"All right, Moira," said Sir. "Just ask Miss Wimpole if she could thp – spare me a minute of her time, please?"

If Miss Wimpole was surprised to find eight people in Sir's office, she didn't show it. As there was no longer room to get inside, she stood at the doorway and waved. Sir waved back. Mike instantly decided that Sir fancied Miss Wimpole.

"Miss Wimpole, I believe you must be the last link in the chain. Am I right in thinking that you wanted June Nichols to see you before assembly, with her red frock?"

"Why, yes," said Miss Wimpole. "She's dancing a solo at the end-of-term concert. I wanted her to practise, but she didn't turn up."

"Thank you," said Sir. "One day, when we both have a spare hour or two, I'll tell you why she didn't turn up. As for you lot," he said, turning to the mob round his desk, "you seem to have been playing Chinese Whispers without knowing it. You also seem to think that the entire staff is off its head. You may be right. I don't know. Red socks, dead dogs, live frogs – we'll put your friend in the school pond, Ruth. Fetch him at break. And now, someone had better find June Nichols and deliver Miss Wimpole's message."

"Oh, there's no point, Sir. She couldn't have come anyway," said Ruth. "She's got chicken-pox. She hasn't been at school for ages."

George Speaks

Dick King-Smith

Laura's baby brother George was four weeks old when it happened.

Laura, who was seven, had very much wanted a brother or sister for a long time. It would be so nice to have someone to play with, she thought. But when George was born, she wasn't so sure.

Everybody – her mother and father, the grandparents, uncles, aunts, friends – made such a fuss of him. And all of them said how beautiful he was. Laura didn't think he was. How could anyone with a round red face and a squashy nose and little tiny eyes all sunken in fat be called beautiful? She looked at him as he lay asleep in his carry-cot.

"Don't wake George up, will you?" her

mother had said. "I'll be in the kitchen if you want me."

"I won't wake you," Laura said to the sleeping baby. "And I don't want to sound rude. But I must tell you something. You look just like a little pig."

And that was when it happened.

The baby opened his eyes and stared straight at her.

"Pig yourself," he said.

Laura gasped. A shiver ran up her spine and her toes tingled.

"What did you say?" she whispered.

"I said, 'Pig yourself'," said George. "You're not deaf, are you?"

"No," said Laura. "No, it's just that I didn't expect you to say anything."

"Why not?"

"Well, babies don't say proper words. They only make noises, like Goo-goo or Blur-blur or Wah."

"Is that a fact?" said the baby.

"Yes," said Laura. "It is. However can you talk like that when you're only four weeks old? It's amazing! I must run and tell Mum."

She turned to dash out of the room.

"Laura!" said the baby sharply.

Laura turned back.

"Yes, George?" she said.

The baby looked at her very severely, his forehead creased into a little frown.

"On no account are you to tell our mother," he said. "Or anyone else for that matter. This is a secret between you and me. Do you understand?"

"Yes, George," said Laura.

"I've been waiting for some time now," said

George, "to speak to you on your own. This is the first proper chance I've had, what with feeding and bathing and nappy-changing and people coming to see me all the time. And talk about making noises – that's all some of them do. They bend over me with silly grins on their faces, and then they come out with a load of rubbish. 'Who's booful den?' 'Who's a georgeous Georgeous Porgeous?' 'Diddums wassums Granny's ickle treasure?' It's an insult to the English language."

"But George," said Laura, "how do you know the English language?"

"Well, I'm English, aren't I?"

"Yes, but how did you learn it?"

"Same way as you, I imagine. Listening to grown-ups talking. I wasn't born yesterday, you know."

"But you're only four weeks old," said Laura. "How did you learn so quickly?"

"I'm a quick learner," said George.

He waved his little arms and kicked his pudgy legs in the air.

"Talking's a piece of cake," he said.

"Trouble is, I haven't learned to control my

body very well yet. In fact, I'm afraid we'll have to postpone the rest of this conversation until another time."

"Why?" asked Laura.

"I'm wet," said George.

"Oh," said Laura. "Shall I go and tell Mummy you need changing?"

"Use your brains, Laura," said George. "You couldn't have known unless I'd told you, could you? You keep quiet. I'll tell her."

"But you said it was going to be a secret between the two of us – you being able to talk, I mean."

"So it is," said George. "I'll tell her in the way she expects. I've got her quite well trained," and he shut his eyes and yelled "Wah! Wah! Wah!" at the top of his voice.

His mother came in.

"What de matter with Mummy's lubbly lickle lambie?" she said.

She picked George up and felt him.

"Oh, he's soaking!" she said. "No wonder he was crying, poor pettikins!"

She smiled at Laura as she changed the baby's nappy. "It's the only way they can let you know there's something wrong, isn't it?" she said.

"Yes, Mummy," said Laura.

She caught George's eye as he lay across his mother's lap. It was no surprise to her that he winked.

For the rest of that day Laura was in a state of great excitement. She kept grinning to herself and hugging herself and doing little dances when no one was looking.

Fancy having a baby brother who could talk! Think of all the things we can talk about, she thought. What a lot there will be for me to tell him! Or will there?

She watched George being bathed, kicking away just like any other small baby, while his mother supported his head with one hand and with the other flicked the warm water over his sticking-out tummy. I shouldn't be surprised, thought Laura, if there's nothing I can tell him. He probably knows it all already.

"He looks clever, doesn't he, Mum?" she said.

"Clever?" said her mother, laughing. "Why he's only a baby, Laura. Babies don't know anything. But he's booful, aren't you, my little ookey-pookey poppet?"

"Gurgle-glug," said George.

Laura didn't get a chance to be alone with George before bedtime. But she spent the whole night, it seemed, dreaming about him.

In one of these dreams she took him to school with her, and carried him into Assembly.

"Laura!" said the headmaster. "That child is far too young to come to school."

"But Sir," said Laura, "he's very intelligent."

"Intelligent, is he?" said the headmaster, while all the children laughed. "I suppose he knows his tables?"

"Of course," Laura said.

The headmaster leaned down towards the baby, who was sitting on Laura's lap. "Well, young man," he said, "perhaps you could tell me the answer to this. What's three times nine?"

"Twenty-seven," said George. He looked scornfully at the headmaster. "I would have expected you to know that," he said.

When Laura woke up next morning and remembered that dream, it seemed fantastic. Fantastic to think that a tiny baby could do sums! Or talk, for that matter. Was *that* all a dream – what she thought had happened yesterday?

"I must make sure," she said, and she jumped out of bed. Peeping round the door of George's room, she saw that he was alone. Mummy was downstairs getting breakfast and Daddy was shaving in the bathroom. Laura went in, closing the door behind her, and looked into the cot.

"George!" she said softly. "It's me, Laura. Listen, George. What's three times nine?"

George smiled at her and waved his fat little hands.

"Goo-goo," he said. "Goo-goo-goo."

Laura's face crumpled. It *had* all been a dream then! She burst into tears.

"Oh, come on, Laura," said George testily. "Don't be such a baby!"

"Oh George!" cried Laura, the tears running down her face. She bent over and kissed the top of his bald head.

"I thought . . .," she said, "I thought . . ."

"I know what you thought," said George. "Can't you take a joke? And do stop crying on me – it's bad enough being wet at the bottom end."

"Sorry," sniffed Laura.

"The answer to your question," said George, "is twenty-seven. Don't you know your tables?"

"Only two times and ten times," said Laura.

George sighed. "I can see you're going to need some help," he said. "Let's start with the three times table. Repeat after me," and he began. "Three ones are three . . ."

They had just finished when the bedroom door suddenly opened and their father came in, rubbing his face with a towel.

"You're a funny old thing, aren't you?" he said to Laura.

"I don't know what you mean," Laura said.

"Well, I was standing outside listening to you say your tables, and you said everything twice over."

"I remember it better that way," Laura said.

"Blur-blur," George said.

"Anyway you got them all right. I didn't know you knew your three times. Clever girl. Wonder if you'll be as clever when you're Laura's age, George?"

"Blur-blur-blur," George said.

Downstairs, the telephone rang.

"It's for you," their mother called, and their father went out of the room.

"Golly!" said Laura. "We nearly gave the game away then! I didn't know Daddy had finished in the bathroom."

George smiled.

"It was a close shave," he said.

The Jelly Custard Surprise

Morris Gleitzman

Rowena Batts communicates by sign language because she can't speak. But she has a step-mother (alias her class teacher, Miss Dunning) whom she likes, a father she adores, and a new baby brother or sister on the way. So what could possibly go wrong at Miss Dunning's leaving party?

I reckon there's something wrong with me.

There must be.

Normal people don't do what I've just done – spoil a wonderful evening and upset half the town and ruin a perfectly good Jelly Custard Surprise.

Perhaps the heat's affected my brain.

Perhaps I've caught some mysterious disease that makes things slip out of my hands.

Perhaps I'm in the power of creatures from another planet who own a lot of dry-cleaning shops.

All I know is ten minutes ago my life was totally and completely happy.

Now here I am, standing in the principal's office, covered in raspberry jelly and lemon custard, waiting to be yelled at and probably expelled and maybe even arrested.

I reckon it was the heat.

It was incredibly hot in that school hall with so many people dancing and talking in loud voices and reaching across each other for the party pies.

And I was running around non-stop, keeping an eye on the ice supply and mopping up spilt drinks and helping Amanda put out the desserts and reminding Dad to play a few waltz records in between the country stuff.

I had to sprint up onto the stage several times to stop the *Farewell Ms Dunning* banner from drooping.

Plus, whenever I saw kids gazing at Ms Dunning and starting to look sad, I'd dash over and stick an apple fritter in their hands to cheer them up.

Every few minutes I went and stood in front of the big fan that Vic from the hardware store had lent for the night, but I still felt like the Murray-Darling river system had decided to give South Australia a miss and run down my back instead.

Amanda was great.

How a person with hair that thick and curly can stay cool on a night like this beats me.

Every time she saw me in front of the fan she gave me a grin.

Don't worry, the grin said, everything's under control and Ms Dunning's having a top time.

That's the great thing about a best friend, half the time you don't even need words.

I'd just given fresh party pies to the principal and the mayor and was heading over to the food table with the bowl of Jelly Custard Surprise when the formalities started. The music stopped and we were all deafened by the screech of a microphone being switched on and the rumble of Amanda's dad clearing his throat.

Amanda's grin vanished.

I gave her a look. Don't panic, it said, once you get up to the microphone you'll be find.

I didn't know if it was true, but I could see it made her feel better.

"Ladies and gentlemen," said Mr Cosgrove, "on behalf of the Parents and Teachers Association Social Committee, it's time for the presentation to our guest of honour."

There was a silence while everyone looked around for Ms Dunning.

She was at the food table, looking startled, gripping Darryn Peck's wrist.

I felt really proud of her at that moment.

There she was, eight and a half months pregnant, hot and weary after spending the whole afternoon making the Jelly Custard Surprise, and she was still taking the trouble to stop Darryn Peck using my apple fritters as frisbees.

No wonder we all think she's the best teacher we've ever had.

Ms Dunning let go of Darryn Peck and went over and stood next to Mr Cosgrove while he made a long speech about how dedicated she is and how sad we all are that she's leaving the school but how we all understand that babies are the future of Australia.

Then Mr Cosgrove called Amanda to the microphone.

She was so nervous she almost slipped over in a drink puddle, but once she was there she did a great job. She read the speech we'd written in her loudest voice without a single mistake, not even during the difficult bit about Ms Dunning being an angel who shone with such radiance in the classroom we hardly ever needed the fluoros on.

After Amanda finished reading she presented Ms Dunning with a carved wooden salad bowl and matching carved wooden fork and spoon which the Social Committee had bought after ignoring my suggestion of a tractor.

Everyone clapped except me because I had my hands full, but I wobbled the Jelly Custard Surprise to show that I would have if I could.

Ms Dunning grinned and blushed and made a speech about how much fun she'd had teaching us and how nobody should feel sad because she'd see everyone most days when she dropped me off at school.

Even though it was a short speech, she was looking pretty exhausted by the time she'd finished.

"I'm pooped," she grinned. "Where's that husband of mine?"

Dad stepped forward and kissed her and she leant on his shoulder and there was more applause.

Dad gave such a big grin I thought his ears were going to flip his cowboy hat off.

I was grinning myself.

Dad's had a hard life, what with Mum dying and stuff, and a top person like him deserves a top person like Ms Dunning.

I reckon marrying Ms Dunning is the best thing he ever did, and that includes buying the apple-polishing machine.

Seeing them standing there, smiling at each other, Ms Dunning smoothing down the fringe on Dad's shirt, I felt happier than I have all year, and I've felt pretty happy for most of it.

Which is why what happened next was so weird.

Dad cleared his throat and went down on one knee so his eyes were level with Ms Dunning's bulging tummy.

I wasn't surprised at that because he does it all the time at home. The mayor, though, was staring at Dad with his mouth open. Mayors get around a fair bit, but they probably don't often come across apple farmers who wear goanna-skin cowboy boots and sing to their wives' tummies.

As usual Dad sang a song by Carla Tamworth, his favourite country and western singer.

It was the one about the long-distance truck driver who listens to tapes of his two-month-old baby crying to keep himself awake while he's driving.

As usual Dad had a bit of trouble with a

few of the notes, but nobody seemed to mind. Ms Dunning was gazing at him lovingly and everyone else was smiling and some people were tapping their feet, including the mayor.

I was enjoying it too, until Dad got to the chorus.

"Your tears are music to my ears," sang Dad to Ms Dunning's midriff, and that's when my brain must have become heat-affected.

Suddenly my heart was pounding and I had a strange sick feeling in my guts.

I turned away.

And suddenly my feet were sliding and suddenly the Jelly Custard Surprise wasn't in my hands anymore.

The bowl still was, but the Jelly Custard Surprise was flying through the air.

It hit the grille of the big hardware store fan, and then everyone in the hall disappeared into a sort of sticky mist. It was just like when Dad sprays the orchard, except his mist isn't pink and it hasn't got bits of custard in it.

I stood there, stunned, while people

shrieked and tried to crawl under the food table.

The mayor still had his mouth open, but now it was full of jelly.

Mr Cosgrove was staring down at his suit in horror, looking like a statue that had just been dive-bombed by a large flock of pink and yellow pigeons.

Darryn Peck was sitting in a Greek salad. I only knew it was him because of the tufts of ginger hair poking up through the sticky pink stuff that covered his face.

I blew the jelly out of my nose and ran out of the hall and thought about hiding in the stationery cupboard but came in here instead.

I'd have ended up here anyway because the principal's office is always where people are taken to be yelled at and expelled and arrested.

There's someone at the door now.

They seem to be having trouble opening it.

It's pretty hard getting a grip on a door handle when you've got Jelly Custard Surprise running out of your sleeves.

I'd help them if I wasn't shaking so much.

The door opened and Mr Fowler came in and it was worse than I'd imagined.

It wasn't just his sleeves that were dripping with jelly and custard, it was most of his shirt and all of his shorts and both knees.

On top of his head, in the middle of his bald patch, were several pieces of pineapple. Ms Dunning always puts crushed pineapple at the bottom of her Jelly Custard Surprise. It's delicious, but it's not really a surprise, not to us. I think it was to Mr Fowler though.

He saw me and just sort of glared at me for a bit.

I tried to stop shaking so I wouldn't drip on his carpet so much.

It was no good. I looked down and saw I was standing in a puddle of passion-fruit topping.

I made a mental note to write to the Department of Education and explain that it had dripped out of my hair and not out of Mr Fowler's lunch box.

Mr Fowler didn't seem to have noticed.

He strode over to his desk and wiped his hands on his blotter.

I waited for him to ring the District Schools Inspector and say, 'I've got a girl here who's been mute since birth and she came to us from a special school fourteen months ago and I thought she was fitting in OK but she's just sprayed two hundred people with Jelly Custard Surprise and so obviously she's not and she'll have to go back to a special school first thing in the morning'.

He didn't.

He just glared at me some more.

"I've seen some clumsy acts in this school,"

he said, "but I think you, Rowena Batts, have just topped the lot."

I didn't reply because my hands were shaking too much to write and Mr Fowler doesn't understand sign language.

"I knew it was a mistake having food," he continued, starting to rummage through the top drawer of his filing cabinet. "That floor was awash with coleslaw from the word go. I nearly slipped over just before you did."

My legs felt like they had jelly on the inside as well as the outside.

"You OK, Tonto?" said a voice from the door.

It was Dad.

His face was creased with concern and splattered with custard, and for a sec I thought he'd changed his shirt. Then I saw it was the blue satin one he'd been wearing all along, but the red jelly had turned it purple.

"I'm fine," I said, trying to keep my hand movements small so I wouldn't flick drips onto Mr Fowler's files.

Ms Dunning came in behind Dad, just as splattered and just as concerned.

She gave me a hug.

"When you have bad luck, Ro, you really have bad luck," she said. "And after all the hard work you put into tonight."

She wiped something off my left elbow, then turned to Mr Fowler.

"We want to get home and cleaned up, Frank," she said. "Can we talk about paying for the damage tomorrow?"

Mr Fowler looked up from the filing cabinet.

"No need," he said, holding up a piece of paper. "The insurance covers accidental food spillage."

Ms Dunning gave such a big sigh of relief that a lump of pineapple slid off the top of her tummy. I caught it before it hit the carpet.

I could tell from Dad's face he wanted to get me out of there before Mr Fowler discovered a clause in the insurance policy excluding jelly.

To get to the truck we had to go through the school hall. It was full of people wiping each other with serviettes and hankies and bits torn off the *Farewell Ms Dunning* banner.

215

I held my breath and hoped they wouldn't notice me.

They did.

People started glowering at me from under sticky eyebrows and muttering things that fortunately I couldn't hear because I still had a fair bit of jelly in my ears.

Amanda came over, her hair rubbed into sticky spikes. "If Mr Fowler tries to murder you," she said with her hands, "tell him to speak to me. I saw you slip."

I felt really proud of her. Not only is she kind and loyal, but I only taught her the sign for 'murder' last week.

"Don't feel bad, Ro," called out Megan O'Donnell's mum, scraping custard off her T-shirt with a knife. "I'm on a diet so I'd rather have it on the outside than on the inside."

There are some really nice people in this town.

But I do feel bad.

I felt bad all the way home in the truck, even though Dad made me and Ms Dunning laugh by threatening to drive us round the orchard on the tractor so all the codling moths would stick to us.

I feel bad now, even though I'm standing under a cool shower.

Because I didn't slip on some coleslaw and accidentally lose control of the Jelly Custard Surprise.

I threw it on purpose.

Hamish Goes Swimming

Humphrey Carpenter

Class Three at St Barty's Primary School were thrilled when their new teacher arrived on the first day of term. Not only did Mr Majeika fly through the window on a magic carpet, he even turned a ruler into a snake and produced chips for everyone. School could never be boring with Mr Majeika in charge!

Mr Magic, as all Class Three were soon calling him, *didn't* forget that he was meant to be a teacher, and not a wizard. Nothing peculiar happened for weeks and weeks, and the lessons went on just as they would have with any other teacher. The magic carpet, the chips, and the snake seemed like a dream.

Then Hamish Bigmore came to stay at Thomas and Pete's house.

This wasn't at all a good thing, at least not for Thomas and Pete. But they had no choice. Hamish Bigmore's mother and father had to go away for a few days and Thomas and Pete's mum had offered to look after Hamish until they came back. She never asked Thomas and Pete what they thought about the idea until it was too late.

Hamish Bigmore behaved even worse than they had expected. He found all their favourite books and games, which they had tried to hide from him, and spoilt them or left them lying about the house where they got trodden on and broken. He pulled the stuffing out of Wim's favourite teddy bear, bounced up and down so hard on the garden climbing-frame that it bent, and talked for hours and hours after the light had been put out at night, so that Thomas and Pete couldn't get to sleep. "It's awful," said Thomas. "I wish that something really nasty would happen to him."

And it did.

Hamish Bigmore was behaving just as badly at school as at Thomas and Pete's house. The business of the ruler turning into a snake had frightened him for a few days, but no longer than that, and now he was up to his old tricks again, doing anything rather than listen to Mr Majeika and behave properly.

On the Wednesday morning before Hamish Bigmore's mother and father were due to come home, Mr Majeika was giving Class Three a nature study lesson, with the tadpoles in the glass tank that sat by his desk. Hamish Bigmore was being ruder than ever.

"Does anyone know how long tadpoles take to turn into frogs?" Mr Majeika asked Class Three.

"Haven't the slightest idea," said Hamish Bigmore.

"Please," said Melanie, holding up her hand, "I don't think it's very long. Only a few weeks."

"*You* should know," sneered Hamish Bigmore. "You look just like a tadpole yourself."

Melanie began to cry.

"Be quiet, Hamish Bigmore," said Mr Majeika. "Melanie is quite right. It all happens very quickly. The tadpoles grow arms and legs, and very soon—"

"I shouldn't think they'll grow at all if they see *you* staring in at them through the glass," said Hamish Bigmore to Mr Majeika. "Your face would frighten them to death!"

"Hamish Bigmore, I have had enough of you," said Mr Majeika. "Will you stop behaving like this?"

"No, I won't!" said Hamish Bigmore.

Mr Majeika pointed a finger at him.

And Hamish Bigmore vanished.

There was complete silence. Class Three stared at the empty space where Hamish Bigmore had been sitting.

Then Pandora Green pointed at the glass tank, and began to shout: "Look! Look! A frog! A frog! One of the tadpoles has turned into a frog!"

Mr Majeika looked closely at the tank. Then he put his head in his hands. He seemed very upset.

"No, Pandora," he said. "It isn't one of the tadpoles. It's Hamish Bigmore."

For a moment, Class Three were struck dumb. Then everyone burst out laughing. "Hooray! Hooray! Hamish Bigmore has been turned into a frog! Good old Mr Magic!"

"It looks like Hamish Bigmore, doesn't it?" Pete said to Thomas. Certainly the frog's expression looked very much like Hamish's face. And it was splashing noisily around the tank and carrying on in the silly sort of way that Hamish did.

Mr Majeika looked very worried. "Oh dear, oh dear," he kept saying.

"Didn't you mean to do it?" asked Jody.

Mr Majeika shook his head. "Certainly not. I quite forgot myself. It was a complete mistake."

"Well," said Thomas, "you can turn him back again, can't you?"

Mr Majeika shook his head again. "I'm not at all sure that I can," he said.

Thomas and Pete looked at him in astonishment.

"You see," he went on, "it was an old spell,

something I learnt years and years ago and thought I'd forgotten. I don't know what were the exact words I used. And, as I am sure you understand, it's not possible to undo a spell unless you know exactly what the words were."

"So Hamish Bigmore may have to stay a frog?" said Pete. "That's the best thing I've heard for ages!"

Mr Majeika shook his head. "For you, maybe, but not for him. I'll have to try and do *something*." And he began to mutter a whole series of strange-sounding words under his breath.

All kinds of things began to happen. The room went dark, and the floor seemed to rock. Green smoke came out of an empty jar on Mr Majeika's desk. He tried some more words, and this time there was a small thunderstorm in the sky outside. But nothing happened to the frog.

"Oh, dear," signed Mr Majeika, "what *am* I going to do?"

Thomas and Pete thought for a moment. Then Thomas said: "Don't worry about it yet,

Mr Magic. Hamish Bigmore's parents are away, and he's staying with us. You've got two days to find the right spell before they come back and expect to find him."

"Two days," repeated Mr Majeika. "In that case there is a chance. We shall simply have to see what happens at midnight."

"Midnight?" asked Jody.

"My friend," said Mr Majeika, "surely you know that in fairy stories everything returns to its proper shape when the clock strikes twelve?"

"Cinderella's coach," said Jody.

"Exactly," answered Mr Majeika. "But one can't be certain of it. There's only a chance. I'll stay here tonight, and see what happens."

And with that, Class Three went home.

Thomas and Pete felt that really they should have taken Hamish Bigmore home with them, even if he *was* a frog. After all, he was supposed to be staying with them.

"But," said Pete, "it's not easy carrying frogs. He might escape, and jump into a river or something, and we'd never see him again."

"And a very good thing too," said Thomas.

"You can't say that," remarked Pete. "He may be only Hamish Bigmore to you and me, but to his mum and dad he's darling little Hamie, or something like that. And just think what it would be like to be mother and father to a frog. Going to the shops, and the library, and that sort of thing, and people saying: 'Oh, Mrs Bigmore, what a *sweet* little frog you're carrying in that jar.' And Hamish's mum having to say: 'Oh, Mrs Smith, that's not just a frog, that's our son, Hamish.'"

When Thomas and Pete's mum saw them at the school gates the first thing she said was "Where's Hamish?", and they had quite a time persuading her that Hamish wouldn't be coming home with them that afternoon, or staying the night, but was visiting friends, and was being perfectly well taken care of.

"Who are these friends?" she asked suspiciously. "What's their name?"

"Tadpoles," said Pete without thinking.

"Idiot," whispered Thomas, kicking him. "We don't know their name," he told his mum. "But Mr Majeika, our new teacher, arranged it, so it must be all right."

"Oh, did he?" said their mum. "Well, he might have told me. But I suppose I shouldn't fuss." And she took them home.

When they got back to school the next morning, Hamish Bigmore was still a frog.

"Nothing happened at all," said Mr Majeika gloomily.

He tried to make Class Three get on with their ordinary work, but it wasn't much use. Nobody had their minds on anything but Hamish Bigmore, swimming up and down in his tank.

Everyone kept making suggestions to Mr Majeika.

"Mr Magic, couldn't you just get a magic wand and wave it over him?"

"Couldn't you say 'Abracadabra' and see if that works?"

"Couldn't you find another wizard and ask him what to do?"

"My friends," said Mr Majeika, "it's no use. There's nothing else to try. Last night, while I was here alone, I made use of every possible means I know, and I can do nothing. And as to finding another wizard, that would be very hard indeed. There are so very few still working, and we don't know each other's names. It might take me years to find another one, and even then he might not have the answer."

Class Three went home rather gloomily that day. They had all begun to feel sorry for Hamish Bigmore. "He's staying with his friends again," Thomas and Pete told their mother.

The next day was Friday. Hamish Bigmore's parents were due to come home that evening.

Half-way through morning school, Jody suddenly put up her hand and said: "Mr Magic?"

"Yes, Jody?"

"Mr Magic, I've got an idea. You said that things *sometimes* happen like they do in fairy stories. I mean, like Cinderella's coach turning back into a pumpkin."

"Yes, sometimes," said Mr Majeika, "but as you've seen with Hamish, not always."

"Well," said Jody, "there is something that I wondered about. You see, in fairy stories people are often turned into frogs. And they always get turned back again in the end don't they? And I've been trying to remember *how*."

Jody paused. "Go on," said Mr Majeika.

"Well," said Jody, "I *did* remember. Frogs turn back into princes when they get kissed by a princess."

Mr Majeika's eyes lit up. "Goodness!" he said. "You're absolutely right! Why didn't I think of that? We must try it at once!"

"Try what, Mr Magic?" asked Pandora Green.

"Why, have Hamish Bigmore kissed by a princess. And then I do believe there's a very good chance he will change back."

"But please, Mr Magic," said Thomas, "how are you going to manage it? I mean, there's not so very many princesses around these days. Not as many as in fairy stories."

"There's some at Buckingham Palace," said Pandora.

"But they don't go around kissing frogs," said Thomas.

"You bet they don't," said Pete. "You see pictures of them in the newspapers doing all sorts of things, opening new hospitals, and naming ships, and that sort of thing. But not kissing frogs."

"Are you sure, my young friend?" said Mr Majeika gloomily.

"Quite sure," said Thomas. "Unless they do it when nobody's looking. I mean, it's not the sort of thing they'd get much fun out of, is it? Frog-kissing, I mean."

"I bet," said Pete, "that a real live princess wouldn't do it if you paid her a thousand pounds."

"Just imagine," said Thomas, "going to Buckingham Palace, and ringing the doorbell, and saying: 'Please, have you got any princesses in today, and would they mind kissing a frog for us?' They'd probably fetch the police."

"Oh dear," said Mr Majeika. "I'm afraid you're right."

Nobody spoke for a long time. Then Mr Majeika said gloomily: "It seems that Hamish Bigmore will have to remain a frog. I wonder what his parents will say."

"Please," said Jody, "I've got an idea again.

It may be silly, but it *might* work. What I think is this. If we can't get a real princess, we might *pretend* to have one. Make a kind of play, I mean. Dress up somebody like a princess. Do you think that's silly?" She looked hopefully at Mr Majeika.

"Not at all," said Mr Majeika. "We've nothing to lose by trying it!"

Which was how Class Three came to spend a good deal of the morning trying to make the room look like a royal palace in a fairy story. They found the school caretaker and persuaded him to lend them some old blue curtains that were used for the play at the end of term. And Mrs Honey who taught the nursery class agreed to give them a box of dressing-up clothes that the little children used. In this were several crowns and robes and other things that could be made to look royal.

Then there was a dreadful argument about who was to play the princess.

Jody said she ought to, because it had all been her idea. Pandora Green said *she* should, because she looked pretty, and princesses always look pretty. Mr Majeika tried to settle it by saying that Melanie should do it, as she was the only girl in the class who hadn't asked to. But Melanie, who hated the idea of kissing a frog, started to cry. So in the end Mr Majeika said that Jody should do it after all, and the other girls could be sort-of-princesses too, only Jody would play the chief one.

Then they got ready. A kind of throne had been made out of Mr Majeika's chair, with one of the blue curtains draped over it. Jody wore another of the curtains as a cloak, and one of the crowns, and a lot of coloured beads from the dressing-up box. And all the other girls stood round her.

Mr Majeika turned out the classroom lights and drew the curtains. Then he said he thought they ought to have some music, just to make things seem more like a fairy story. So Thomas got out his recorder, and played 'God Save the Queen' and 'Good King Wenceslas', which were the only tunes he knew. They didn't seem quite right for the occasion, but Mr Majeika said they would have to do. Then he told Jody to start being the princess, and say the sort of things that princesses might say in fairy stories.

Jody thought for a moment. Then she said in a high voice: "O my courtiers, I have heard that in this kingdom there is a poor prince who has been enchanted into a frog by some wicked magician." She turned to Mr Majeika and whispered: "You're not wicked, really, Mr Magic, but that's what happens in fairy stories, isn't it?"

"Of course," said Mr Majeika. "Please continue. You are doing splendidly."

"O my courtiers," went on Jody, "I do request that one of you shall speedily bring me this frog. For I have seen it written that should a princess of the blood royal kiss this poor frog with her own lips, he will regain his proper shape." She paused. "Well, go on, somebody," she hissed. "Fetch me the frog!"

It was Mr Majeika himself who stepped up to the tank, put in his hands, and drew out Hamish Bigmore. So he did not see the door opening and Mr Potter coming into the room.

"Ah, Mr Majeika," said Mr Potter, "I just

wanted to ask you if you could look after school dinner again today, because—" He stopped, staring at the extraordinary scene.

Mr Majeika was kneeling on one knee in front of Jody, holding out the frog. "Go on," he whispered, "I feel the magic working."

"O frog," said Jody in her high voice, "O frog, I command you, turn back into a prince!" And she kissed the frog.

"Now, really," said Mr Potter, "I'm not at all in favour of nature study being mixed up with story-times. And school curtains should not be used for this sort of thing. While as to that

frog, its proper place is a pond. I'll allow tadpoles in school, but not frogs. They jump out of the tanks and get all over the place. Now, if you'll just hand that one over . . . Where is it?"

"Here I am," said Hamish Bigmore. He had appeared out of nowhere, and the frog was gone.

Mr Potter sat down very suddenly in the nearest chair. "I don't feel very well," he said.

"Ah," said Hamish Bigmore, "you should try being a frog for a few days. Does you no end of good. Makes you feel really healthy, I can tell you. All that swimming about, why, I've never felt better in my life. And being kissed by princesses, too. Not that my princess was a real one." He turned to Mr Majeika. "You really should have taken me to Buckingham Palace," he said. "I'm sure the Queen herself would have done it, to oblige me."

Mr Potter got to his feet and left the room, muttering something about needing to go and see a doctor because he was imagining things.

"And now," said Hamish Bigmore to Class Three, "I'm going to tell you all about the life and habits of the frog." Which he did, at great length.

"Oh dear," said Pete to Thomas. "He's worse than ever."

ACKNOWLEDGEMENTS

The publishers wish to thank the following for permission to reproduce copyright material:

Paul Jennings: "UFD" from *Uncanny!*, by Paul Jennings; first published by Penguin Australia Ltd 1988 and reproduced with their permission.

Norman Hunter: "Count Bakwerdz on the Carpet" from *Count Bakwerdz on the Carpet and Other Incredible Stories* by Norman Hunter; first published by The Bodley Head 1979 and reproduced by permission of Random House UK Ltd.

Anne Fine: "Good News Bear" from *How to Write Really Badly* by Anne Fine; first published my Methuen Children's Books 1996 and reproduced by permission of Reed Consumer Books Ltd.

P L Travers: "Laughing Gas" from *Mary Poppins* by P L Travers; first published by HarperCollins 1958, revised 1982 and reproduced by permission of David Higham Associates.

Clement Freud: "Monday" from *Grimble* by Clement Freud; first published by HarperCollins 1968 and reproduced by permission of the author, Sir Clement Freud.

Anthony Buckeridge; "Burnt Offering" from *Speaking of Jennings* by Anthony Buckeridge; first published by HarperCollins 1973 and by Macmillan Children's Books 1996 and reproduced by permission of the author.

Judy Blume: "Who's the Lucky Bride?" from *Fudge-a-Mania* by Judy Blume; first published in the UK by The Bodley Head 1990 and in the USA by Dutton Children's Books 1990 and reproduced by permission of Random House UK Ltd and Dutton Children's Books, a division of Penguin Books USA Inc.

Eva Ibbotson: "Not Just a Witch", an extract from *Not Just a Witch* by Eva Ibbotson; first published by Macmillan Children's Books 1989 and reproduced by permission of the author.

Judy Corbalis: "The Enchanted Toad" from *The Wrestling Princess and Other Stories* by Judy Corbalis; first published by Andre Deutsch 1984 and reproduced by permission of Scholastic Children's Books.

David Henry Wilson: "How Not to be a Giant Killer" from *There's a Wolf in my Pudding* by David Henry Wilson; first published by J.M. Dent and reproduced by permission of The Orion Publishing Group Ltd.

ACKNOWLEDGEMENTS

James Berry: "Mrs Anancy, Chicken Soup and Anancy" from *Anancy Spiderman* by James Berry; text copyright © 1988 James Berry, originally illustrated by Joseph Olubo; first published by Walker Books Ltd 1988 and reproduced with their permission.

Jan Mark: "Send Three and Fourpence We Are Going to a Dance" from *Nothing To Be Afraid Of* by Jan Mark, copyright © Jan Mark 1977, 1980; first published by Kestrel Books 1980 and reproduced by permission of Penguin Books Ltd.

Dick King-Smith: "George Speaks", an extract from *George Speaks* by Dick King-Smith, copyright © Dick King-Smith 1988; first published by Viking 1988 and reproduced by permission of Penguin Books Ltd.

Morris Gleitzman: "The Jelly Custard Surprise", an extract from *Sticky Beak* by Morris Gleitzman; first published in Australia by Pan Macmillan Publishers 1993 and in the UK by Macmillan Children's Books 1994 and reproduced by permission of the author.

Humphrey Carpenter: "Hamish Goes Swimming" from *Mr Majeika* by Humphrey Carpenter, copyright © Humphrey Carpenter 1984; first published by Kestrel Books 1984 and reproduced by permission of Penguin Books Ltd.

Funny stories

for 5 Year Olds

Chosen by Helen Paiba

A bright and varied selection of wonderfully entertaining stories by some of the very best writers for children. Perfect for reading alone or aloud – and for dipping into time and time again. With stories from Dick King-Smith, Tony Ross, Alf Prøysen, Malorie Blackman and many more, this book will provide hours of fantastic fun.

Funny Stories for 6 Year Olds

Chosen by Helen Paiba

A bright and varied selection of wonderfully
entertaining stories by some of the very
best writers for children. Perfect for
reading alone or aloud — and for dipping
into time and time again. With stories from
Margaret Mahy, David Henry Wilson, Francesca
Simon, Tony Bradman and many more,
this book will provide hours of fantastic fun.

Funny
stories

for
7
year olds

Chosen by Helen Paiba

A bright and varied selection of wonderfully
entertaining stories by some of the very
best writers for children. Perfect for reading
alone or aloud – and for dipping into time
and time again. With stories from Dick
King-Smith, Michael Bond, Philippa Gregory,
Jacqueline Wilson and many more,
this book will provide hours of fantastic fun.

Tom Percival

Little Legends

THE SPELL THIEF

Welcome to
Tale Town!

Life for Jack is great – he's got a magical talking hen called Betsy, he lives in a town where stories *literally* grow on trees, and all his best friends live there with him. That is, until new kid in town, Anansi, arrives . . .

When Jack sees Anansi having a secret meeting with a troll – *everything* changes. Trolls mean trouble and Jack will stop at *nothing* to prove that Tale Town is in danger. Even if that means using stolen magic!

Download the
FREE app
LITTLE LEGENDS
RACE DAY
at littlelegends.club

They may be small, but their adventures are epic!

Little Legends are also available from

Me Books

•ELLI WOOLLARD•

Swashbuckle Lil

The Secret Pirate

Two brilliantly
illustrated rhyming
stories!

ILLUSTRATED BY LAURA ELLEN ANDERSON

Lil is a pirate, a good sort of pirate,
And when there is someone to save,
She'll do what is right (if it takes her all night).
Yes, she'll always be bold and be brave.

When evil pirate Stinkbeard tries to kidnap Lil's teacher, it's
up to schoolgirl and secret pirate, Lil, to come to the rescue.

In story two it's sports day, but there's a very hungry croc
on the loose. Can Lil and her trusty parrot, Carrot,
scare Stinkbeard and his pet croc away?